ASYLUM

*asylum (n), institution for the insane; alt.
haven, a place of safety*

**A Journey
From Innocence**

BY

Hugo Thal

ISBN: 1-4033-3376-9 (Electronic)
ISBN: 1-4033-3377-7 (Softcover)

Library of Congress Control Number:
2002092122

This book is printed on acid free
paper.

Printed in the United States of
America
Bloomington, IN

1stBooks - rev. 10/22/02

For Kate, Karen, Danielle and Lauren
Children of apartheid. Now free

AUTHOR'S NOTE

This story is based on fact. Most of the people mentioned are still alive and living in South Africa. To protect the privacy of those individuals who have not been approached for permission to use their names in the context of this story, pseudonyms have been substituted where necessary.

CONTENTS

INTRODUCTION

Like South Africa itself, answers to questions about what it was like living in that country are complex. It was ordinary. And extraordinary.

While the wrenching experience of fleeing to seek political asylum in the United States added more layers of ambiguity to my feelings about the land of my birth, the underlying confusion that lay buried deep in my soul was probably little different from that experienced by most white South Africans. We loved the place. And we hated it. Sometimes the things we loved and the things we hated were interchangeable. The intimate co-existence of First World and Third World cultures in a land that was at once sophisticated and untamed, wildly unpredictable yet delicately beautiful, savage and sensitive, provided a rich smorgasbord from which we drew experiences that were unique, unforgettable, exhilarating and deeply troubling, sometimes all at once.

South Africa was many things to many people: it was seldom dull.

Fertile seeds for my personal confusion were sown long before I was born. My mother, a minor pillar of Cape Town society, traced her ancestry back to Dutch and French forebears who settled the southern tip of Africa in 1670. She was raised, like others of similar descent, to believe passionately that hers were a people anointed through a special covenant with God to rule and civilize the land. Thus, to her, apartheid was not a self-serving political aberration but a divine commission.

My father's parents were German Jewish immigrants who arrived relatively late on the scene, in 1890, and quickly assimilated the prevailing wisdom of the white community.

Yet despite their roots and the deep antipathy my parents shared towards the British colonial power, my father volunteered to fight in the Second World War on the side of the British, against the Germans. And from a young age I was sent to join my brother at a very proper English boarding school located in a bleak little town hundreds of miles from our home, where we were taught to venerate the British Empire.

Added to these inconsistencies were wildly conflicting signals about racial attitudes. While my parents held to the prevailing view that black people were inherently inferior, rightly consigned by law to a second-class status, much of my father's business depended on cordial relations with black customers and in his dealings with them he was completely colorblind. He often broke with convention by accepting invitations to dine in black homes or to occasionally stay the night in the home of a black friend when he found himself in a remote area. Indeed, when he later prepared me to take over his business he stressed that continued thoughtful and generous treatment of his black customers was essential, at a time when racial attitudes were hardening on both sides of the color line.

On the other hand, it was unthinkable for my parents to invite a black person into our home, unless it was as a servant.

These were the irreconcilable impressions that shaped my destiny and brought so much conflict into my life during the latter years of my stay in South Africa. Now as I look back on that time from the vantage point of a peaceful and prosperous life in America I wonder at the fates which conspired to plant me there before bringing me here. No doubt, that thought is shared by thousands of South Africans - mostly whites but also some blacks - who left their homes in the last 15 or 20 years to start new lives in host countries on every continent.

I chose America simply because my older brother was already here. A successful marketing executive who traveled widely overseas during the 1980s, he foresaw South Africa's self-destruction before others in his circle were ready to acknowledge it and traded his comfortable lifestyle for a job in London, England, before accepting a marketing vice president's position in the United States and settling here in 1990. Four years later when I arrived with my family we joined him in Albuquerque, New Mexico, where he was living at the time.

It is fitting that we should collaborate in the writing of this book because our widely varied yet often surprisingly similar experiences complement each other and confirm details that we might otherwise doubt, if for no other reason than that they are so foreign to our present experience, like a dream viewed through the wrong end of a telescope.

Thus, while the vehicle for this story is the harrowing trial in which I had to prove my eligibility for political asylum in the United States, our shared memories provide much of the material that appears in the form of recollections and impressions of a life and a time and a place that is gone forever; a season of innocence and awakening in a land that seems to have had more than its fair share of opportunities and disasters.

And having sacrificed so much to escape those disasters, we are also keenly sensitive to currents in the American political landscape that seem to have the potential to tear this great nation apart. A growing emphasis on group identity at the expense of individual identity (the very philosophy that lay at the root of the odious apartheid system) threatens a descent into a form of tribalism that bodes ill for the future. Multiculturalism, for all its politically correct connotations, offers nothing more than a choice of balkanization over the cultural melting pot that has brought unparalleled unity and prosperity to America. As more and more racial, social and special-interest groups stake their claim to a bias in their favor based on real or imagined perceptions of their unique collective rights, we see the whole cloth of American society beginning to unravel strand by strand, and we wonder anew at the strange fate that may cause us to be witnesses of the agony this brings, not once, but twice in our lifetimes. Perhaps this book may play a small part in helping to avoid such a fate.

Extracts From A Letter
Written in Support of a Petition for Political Asylum
February 28, 1995.

"Phillip H. Thal is my brother. About a year ago he left South Africa to seek asylum in the United States. In so doing he left behind all he had and all he had known - his home, friends, his wife's mother and a thriving business that had enabled him to accumulate several million dollars worth of assets. All of this was forsaken.

"The circumstances leading to such a drastic and painful choice were themselves drastic. Phillip's life was in very real danger due to active political, moral and financial support of the African National Congress (now the party in power in South Africa).

"To appreciate the threat to his life then, and the very real threat that remains now, despite a favorable change of government, it is necessary to understand the particular society in which he lived, and his courageous actions there on behalf of oppressed black people.

"Phillip's home was in an area even more conservative on racial issues than the rest of South Africa. A U.S. equivalent would be a comparison between 1950's racial attitudes in New York City with Birmingham, Alabama.

"Phillip's was a lone white voice speaking out on behalf of his black friends, employees and political colleagues, in a rural backwater where it was unheard of for whites to view blacks as anything more than "hewers of wood and drawers of water" (an actual phrase from what was until recently official government policy towards so-called non-whites).

"The principled attitude and actions of this lone white man stirred deep divisions and fierce hatreds in his community, such that no change of government could alleviate the threats he still faces. Indeed, it is possible that the triumph of the African National Congress at the polls, long overdue, has heightened the threat to Phillip because there will be many disgruntled whites in his former home who view him as the traitor who made their defeat sure.

"It may be years before these harsh judgements of him abate. Until then, any return by him to the community which he served so well and so unselfishly, would seal his fate…

"I am proud of my brother and what he stood for. As a permanent resident of the United States I am equally proud of what this country stands for and the salvation and security it offers to people like my brother."

Edward H. Thal.

CHAPTER ONE
Escape

I remember every detail of the moment I was told my time had come to die.

It was a day in April, and it was late. The voice on the other end of the phone was strained, hushed: "Phillip? Listen...I'm only going to say this once. I owe you; you saved my life. This is payback."

There was a pause, and I could hear soft breathing.

"Who is this?"

"Man, just listen!"

"Rolf, is that you?"

It took a few seconds to match a face with the lowered voice. Roelof Botha. A sometime friend who had been avoiding me for the past three or four years, like so many others. Rolf. Yes, of course: there was a time when his business was failing, and I bailed him out. We were closer then; his daughters had been best friends with my two girls, and I think I did it mainly for them. I liked the sound of their happy laughter around my house.

A month after Rolf got back on his feet, he told me that he had come very close to suicide. "You saved my life, man!" I remember him saying in that rough way of his. Now here he was on the phone, sounding almost ill.

"Rolf?"

"Man...Phillip, just shut up and listen! They took a vote last night." He paused. "The next bullet's for you, man."

"For you."

"Phillip, this is no joke. You're dead!"

The crawling sensation down my spine surprised me: I thought that happened only in novels. I had been scared before; fear was a constant companion, the last three years, but this was different.

"Rolf?"

He was gone.

Taking the phone from my ear, I stared dumbly at its hard black surface, struggling to make sense of the call. Was it genuine? Who, or what, was behind it? Did Rolf not know, or care, that the security police tapped my phone? Or did the security police put him up to it? Perhaps it was just another threat? There had been threats, many threats: phone calls, graffiti on my walls, a small bomb thrown at my house, late at night, and some shots fired, but that was just intimidation; everybody understood it was part of the game -chicken - who would blink first? Yet this was different. The stress in Rolf's voice was real. The feeling of impending disaster that had oppressed me the last few months was real.

The sick feeling in the pit of my stomach told me I had just blinked.

The horror of John's murder was too raw for me to ignore Rolf's call. John had died like an animal: one bullet, in the back of the head, execution-style. Now they were coming after me. So soon! I had badly miscalculated their determination, their anger. My friend had paid with his life because I had foolishly agreed with him that he was too unimportant to be targeted, but he was my final warning, written in blood. I saw his face in front of me, open, smiling, hopeful, and the sick feeling inside me grew overpowering. John was the younger brother of my business partner, David, yet so unlike David whose interests, like most white South Africans, were firmly fixed on beer, barbecues and golf. David viewed me as half-crazed because of my activist support for the African National Congress, but John was fascinated by my stand, eager to learn more. We spent long hours discussing South Africa's political landscape, and at last he became committed to the struggle for freedom from the oppressive apartheid system. I wasn't actively recruiting him, but in my loneliness I had found his enthusiasm appealing and I did nothing to discourage him as his awareness grew and the intensity of his emotions sometimes caused him to boil over in anger at the injustices that occurred routinely on his behalf, as a privileged member of the white ruling class, against others who were for the most part helpless to resist and who found it impossible to hide from the heavy hand of oppression because their skin color branded them indelibly with the curse of inferiority. John was aware of the dangers, of course. Back in the early '90s it was not yet fashionable to support the recently unbanned ANC, not if you had a white skin, and especially not if you lived in a small country town where there were no isolated corners in which to safely express your allegiance to Nelson Mandela's despised organization. As soon as you declared yourself, however mildly, in word or deed, your leprosy became known to the entire white community.

But I had survived the shunning and the derision, the threats and the intimidation's, and John was confident he could also. He understood, and he was not afraid, he said.

Now he was dead. Too late, I recognized his fatal weakness: he was expendable. His death would not create much of a ripple, but it would act as a stark warning to me and others like me who were perceived as traitors to their white heritage. Initially I gave no outward sign that I was intimidated. I felt I owed it to John to continue, and to the many other unsung martyrs who had given their lives in the struggle for freedom. The decision did not take much thought: I had survived so long, against all the odds, and had become so entrenched in my political views, that each new crisis, and this crisis in particular, merely strengthened my resolve. Besides, I drew comfort from the knowledge that I was now so well known in my small corner of the universe that my death, unlike John's, would stir up a hornet's nest of mass protests, strikes, media scrutiny, demands for justice, and more than a cursory attempt to apportion blame. It was the same harsh reality, on a much larger scale, that kept Mandela alive.

And yet…John's death had scared me more than I wanted to admit. And now, faced with the chilling authenticity of Rolf's brief telephone call, I had at last to confront the fact that I too was expendable. I was no Nelson Mandela, just a small-town white businessman who had risen to become vice chairman of the local chapter of the African National Congress. For some in my community this shocking betrayal and its many concomitant traitorous deeds had finally become intolerable.

The next bullet was for me. The awful certainty of it settled on me like a shroud.

I took a deep breath, and thought of Linda and the kids, upstairs in bed. Warm. Safe. Vulnerable. Their lives literally hung on my decisions and the actions I took as a consequence of those decisions. Life. Or death. Yet I reminded myself that in the scenario I now faced, no rushed decision was necessary - it had been made months ago after a petrol bomb was thrown at our house. Linda had given me an ultimatum. The bomb was small and ineffective, nobody was home at the time, and little real damage was done. But Linda was adamant: she had just returned from a short stay with her mother, but this time she was leaving for good, and taking the kids with her, unless I could give her an absolute assurance that their lives were not in danger.

"Honey, you were never in danger because you weren't even at home," I replied.

"Oh, damn you!" she shot back. "I know that! But what if I had been at home? What if the children had been right at the spot where the bomb landed? What then?"

"Don't be silly," I said softly, choosing my words with care, "you know I can't answer hypothetical questions like that. The fact is, nobody was home, and the bomb was not really intended to hurt anybody. It was just a message, a warning. If people really wanted to hurt us, don't you think they would have done so?"

There was an awkward silence as Linda stared at me, her gaze uncomprehending.

"How can you do this?" she finally asked, shaking her head. "How can you sit there and calmly tell me that people who throw bombs at our house don't want to hurt us? How can you gamble like this with the lives of your children, with my life, with your own life? Isn't it time to admit that you're in over your head, that this political stuff is way out of control and nothing is going to be resolved until everybody in this insane country has killed everybody else?"

She was shouting now, and I could see the fear in her eyes. But there was something else there, something I had not seen before - doubt. Linda had always trusted my judgement. She had been loyal and supportive through the years of my slow metamorphosis from political spectator to political activist although her views on the remedy for the injustices endemic to our society were very different from my own. But whatever her political stance, she was first a wife and mother. She was the one who stayed home and watched the children while I led the protest marches; she was the one who endured the hostility at the supermarket while I was at another ANC committee meeting; and it was she who comforted the children when their school friends said cruel things to them. In many ways, the toll had been greater on her than on me, yet she had always trusted that I would make the right choices, not only for the political cause to which I was committed, but especially for my family. Now, with scorch marks still discernable on the wall of our home from the bomb that had landed nearby, she was doubting me. She saw my cause as hollow: I wanted to help save South Africa at the cost of losing those who were dearest to me.

I reached out and drew her close as I spoke the words that presaged this day of my death sentence: "Linda. I love you. I love our children. And I'll make you this solemn promise: the day I believe our lives really are in danger, we'll go. We'll get away from all this."

She did not reply, and my mind was racing as I studied the implications of what I had just said. Her continued silence unnerved me; clearly, she remained doubtful. So I added: "Look, to prove I really mean this, I'll begin planning right now for us to leave. The day might never come, but if it does, we'll be ready."

At last, she spoke. "Where will we go?"

Where would we go? The world was a big, lonely place, and I suddenly saw how complete our isolation was, in this hostile country on the tip of Africa, a hostile continent in a hostile world where my white South African skin branded me as a pariah.

With a confidence I did not feel, I replied, "To America. My brother's been nagging me for years to join him there. He says it really is a land of opportunity where we can make a new start, and it has laws that protect people like us if we arrive as refugees."

"Refugee?" my wife said, rolling the word off her tongue. "Refugee. It sounds awful, like something to do with war or famine. Why can't we just emigrate like other people do?"

"Honey," I replied, in a weak attempt at humor, "if we have to make a run for it, it will be war!"

But Linda wasn't laughing, so I explained: "There are many reasons why it would be almost impossible for us to emigrate. Firstly, the South African Government makes it very difficult for people like us to leave, with our white skins and our white skills and our white money. The legal process and the tax scrutiny and the financial restrictions are a nightmare.

In a real sense, we're prisoners here, held by golden chains. And even if we decide to break those chains, we have to find a place to go, a place that will accept us. That means I need a firm job offer in a foreign country, based on unique or highly technical skills which I don't have; or we must have close relatives who are citizens of that country, who will petition for our entry there. And either process - leaving here and getting in there - could drag on for years. In the meantime, everybody here will know we're planning to get out, and if you think we're treated like skunks now, our life would become unbearable then. We'd be rejected by both whites and blacks, and there's no telling where the bullet with my name on it will come from then!"

That was several months ago. As I stood there now in the darkness of my sleeping home, still clutching the telephone, holding onto it almost to steady myself, I ran through a mental checklist of my careful preparations since that fateful day when the thought of actually leaving South Africa had become a concrete possibility. My first act, to make my commitment real to Linda, was to buy four matching suitcases, one for each of us, and tell her to begin packing!

"Imagine we're leaving next month," I said, "and these suitcases are all we can take. Pack everything we're going to need to live with for two weeks. Then we'll store the cases so that when it's time to go we can literally just pick them up and walk out the door. Think about your choices very carefully. Every item will have to be packed for a reason. And don't forget the photo albums!"

I should have avoided that last reference. Linda had listened attentively to my instructions, all businesslike, until I mentioned the albums. Then she burst into tears.

"I can't do this," she sobbed. "You want me to pack our whole life into four miserable little suitcases!"

She waved her hand around the bedroom. "Look around you, Phillip, there's enough just in this one room to fill a small truck."

"Yes. But we don't need it all. Pack what we need. You're going to have to make some tough choices, but I know you can do it."

Linda sighed, then she smiled weakly and said, "Well, I suppose it will take my mind off the fact that some idiot might throw another bomb at us."

The project worked so well that when "some idiot" did fire shots at our home a few weeks later, Linda took it in her stride. She had something to hold onto now: the hope that soon we would leave this craziness behind us.

My next challenge was to get my hands on some money. Real money. To prevent the flight of capital to safer havens overseas, there were severe limitations on the amount of money that could legally be taken out of the country, and the penalty for being caught smuggling currency was the confiscation of everything you owned. People who were rich enough and desperate enough to leave South Africa got around these restrictions by setting up dummy corporations overseas and double-billing for goods or services. Others simply sank their life savings into fancy yachts and sailed off to find a buyer in the foreign port of their choice. I chose the relatively less complicated route of buying United States dollars on the black market. In the back of my mind I had the idea that I would find a way to stuff the linings of our four suitcases with $100 bills. As it turned out this was a dangerously wrong assumption, but in the meantime I occupied myself with the delicate task of locating dollars through a wide network of business contacts, buying a little at a time from a variety of sources so as not to excite too much attention to what I was doing. It was a tedious and very expensive procedure, with each unit of U.S. currency costing me about four units of my own currency.

I thought about the money now, tightly rolled scraps of paper buried in cans of talcum powder, some $31,000 in all. The unusual form of storage was the result of research on my part that revealed how easy it was for airport scanners to detect large amounts of contraband money from the signals given off by tiny silver strips printed onto the bills. A masking agent was needed and the innocent aluminum cans of talcum powder, one in each suitcase, would do the job nicely. But when I first uncovered this fact it scared me into wondering what else I had overlooked or simply taken for granted in my amateurish approach to planning an escape, and my heightened fear of exposure caused me to break off further attempts to buy dollars. The $31,000 would have to do. Added to $7,000 apiece that Linda and I were legally allowed to take out of the country, the total of $45,000 was a depressingly small return on a lifetime of hard work that had given me a net worth of several million dollars, and it was hardly enough to start a new life in a strange country. But I consoled myself with the thought that it was a lot more than the average boat person had when he stepped ashore on the Florida Keys.

Our mode of transport to the U.S. would be somewhat more high-tech than a leaky old rowing boat, but in many other ways my family and I would be "boat people" - alienated from our home, desperate, fearful, trusting only in the mercy of the United States Government. Of course, until we declared our intention to seek political asylum there, we would simply be arriving as happy tourists. Everything was in place to make that happen.

John's death four months prior to Rolf's chilling telephone call had spurred me to buy "open" airline tickets to America, good for one year. It helped Linda's peace of mind to show her that we had actual tickets, and my reasoning was that if we did not use them in the next twelve months, I would simply turn them in for a refund. At the same time I applied to the American embassy for visas, stating that the purpose was to take our daughters on a vacation to Disneyland. With remarkably good timing, the visas had arrived just a week ago.

Fortunately, passports were not a problem because our location on the border of Lesotho - the tiny independent kingdom tucked away in the heart of South Africa - and my business interests there meant that the possession of current travel documents was a way of life for us. I crossed the border each week, sometimes several times a week, while Linda and the children often accompanied me for short vacations or visits to friends. Indeed, Lesotho was such a convenient neighbor, with its border literally only minutes from the door of our home, that Linda had suggested fleeing there for safety if the time ever came when we had to leave in a hurry. But Lesotho was too close, too small and too weak to resist the touch of death from South African hit squads who operated almost with impunity in that country.

No, if we were going to escape, and stay alive, we would have to go far away.

Now, as if in a dream, I had to confront the fact that it was time to do just that. Relinquishing my iron grip on the telephone at last, I made my way slowly through the darkened house, suddenly overwhelmed by a deep sadness. Everything I loved and wanted was right here; my family asleep in their comfortable bedrooms upstairs, the spacious downstairs entertainment area, the large kitchen where I enjoyed creating the occasional gourmet meal, the workout room, the jacuzzi, the big colorful garden beyond the large patio doors. My entire life was here, the carefree laughter of my children, the tapestry of a thousand conversations with Linda and our friends, the myriad small details that made up the whole cloth of our existence, all woven into the very air around me.

And I was about to take a step that would separate me forever from it all.

Could I do it? Now that the thing I feared had suddenly come upon me, I felt weak, frail, unsure. The enormity of my decision was a crushing weight as I saw with a sudden sharp clarity how the irrevocable steps we would take in the next hours would forever change the course of our lives. An incongruous thought came to me unbidden, and I blurted it out aloud: "My grandchildren will be foreigners!"

I smiled ruefully at the picture in my mind, and then added for good measure, "Yes, idiot boy: and you'll never watch rugby again, and you'll never go skiing in the Maluti Mountains again, and you'll never get chased by a rhino again. So wad'dya want?"

What I wanted was to stay alive! Ignoble and unsettling as it was to flee, the alternative of a shabby, untimely death was profoundly hollow. I was satisfied that I had done all I could, risked all I could, given all I could: my forty years in South Africa had not been wasted. But now it was time to go.

I found myself standing at our bedroom door. Taking a deep breath, I gently pushed it open and walked in. Linda was awake, reading.

"Who called?" she asked, looking at me over the top of her book.

I couldn't speak. Recognition dawned in her eyes as she deciphered the stricken look on my face, and suddenly she was standing beside me, holding me.

"Phillip, talk to me, what's happened?"

I struggled to compose myself, to suppress my anxiety. But my voice was hoarse as I answered: "It's time to go."

The words hung in the air between us; alien, harsh. Thankfully, Linda said nothing. She knew, she had known for a long time this day would come. Again and again she had played the scene over in her mind, and she told me later that when it happened it came almost as an anti-climax. She asked a few brief questions and then we sat quietly on the bed, side-by-side. Finally, with a long sigh, she leaned her head on my shoulder.

"When do you want to leave?"

For a question that carried such profound implications, it was incongruous in its simplicity. I answered without emotion.

"Early in the morning. We need to get a few hours sleep, then we'll pack the car. I'll help you get the kids ready. Then we'll wake the maids and tell them we've decided to take a quick vacation. The weekend's coming up and we've done this before so they won't sense anything out of the ordinary. I want to be on the road by sunrise."

"I should call and say goodbye to my mother."

"No! Listen, Linda, we've discussed all this. We can't take the risk. We can't tell anybody. Not until we're in America. Not until we're safe. Don't wimp out on me now; we've both got to be strong."

Linda gave a hollow laugh as she replied, "Don't worry. I'm not going to do anything foolish. I just felt it was the right thing to say. Your parents are both dead and my mother's our only surviving blood link to this country; it just seems so cold-hearted to walk away without so much as a little goodbye. But," she turned to me and smiled, "I do understand, really I do. We'll call her when we're safely in America."

I looked down at her, snuggled into my shoulder, and I felt a deep love for her well up inside me.

"Have I ever told you that I think you're amazing?" I said quietly.

"Not often enough!" she replied.

Five hours later, with the early morning sun lighting the way ahead we were on our way to Johannesburg, 300 miles to the north. Two sleepy children lay cuddled together on the back seat; in the trunk, four carefully-packed suitcases and two shoulder bags contained all our worldly possessions. Neither Linda nor I spoke much; we were both lost in our own thoughts, watching the familiar landscape pass by for the last time.

I wasn't afraid. Our departure had come so quickly in response to Rolf's warning that I doubted anyone would have anticipated it. By the time the hit squad completed its preparations to come after us, we would be long gone! This was exactly as I had foreseen it would have to be; once the decision was made to go, there was no sense in waiting. In retrospect, I was deeply grateful that Linda had been so adamant about taking the threats to our lives seriously after that ineffective little bomb was thrown. At the time the prospect of being intimidated enough to contemplate flight was personally so remote that I never would have begun planning for such an eventuality. And now, because of our careful planning, we had an excellent chance of making a clean escape.

We arrived in Johannesburg after an uneventful five-hour drive and checked into a hotel near the airport. I immediately called the airline and found there were seats available on a flight leaving the next afternoon. Then there was nothing to do but wait.

Shortly after leaving our home, I had called David from a public telephone to tell him we would be going away for a few days. I would call him again from the United States to let him know the few days might be forever! All the paperwork relating to the business, including a power-of-attorney for David to act on my behalf, was prepared and waiting for him at my lawyer's office.

Among the papers was a letter to David explaining my actions, and a second letter for the servants at our home. That letter contained details of a pension I had left for both of them. Hopefully, the house would be sold in the not-too-distant future, at a reasonable price, and the proceeds would be used to finance some remaining small obligations. But perhaps the house would be confiscated. I wasn't sure about the legal position and had resisted the temptation to seek counsel on the subject from my lawyer: he was a man of principle and we had been friends for many years, but I had remained firm in my resolve that absolutely no-one should have even the slightest indication that we were planning to leave the country. So, for the moment, Linda and I had simply turned out the lights in our home and walked out the door, both of us resisting the temptation to look back as the car headed out of the driveway.

There were just two hurdles left. Both were so fraught with danger that I had resisted thinking about them, but now that they lay immediately ahead I could avoid them no longer. First, we had to safely negotiate customs and passport control before we boarded the aircraft to leave South Africa; and assuming that went off without a hitch, the second hurdle was entrance into America. Of the two, the first undoubtedly posed the greatest threat. South African border control officials were notoriously tough - always on the lookout for real and imagined spies, terrorists and currency smugglers - and I had no way of knowing if they had my name on some sort of secret list of undesirable political activists who were potential or actual enemies of the State. Worse, I did not know how closely connected my intended executioners were to the state security police, whose tentacles stretched everywhere and who might already have sent out an alert for my apprehension or arrest.

As I contemplated this prospect I wondered for the hundredth time who, precisely, had decided to kill me? Was it a freelance operation by a group of hometown fanatics who had lost patience with my seeming immunity to intimidation, or was it the shadowy Third Force? The existence of this latter group was only rumored at the time, but the rumors were grounded on so much circumstantial evidence that everyone took them to be fact. Indeed, years later South Africa's so-called Truth Commission confirmed that they were members of the security forces acting behind the scenes but with the sanction of high-placed South African Government officials. The polite term was that they acted in an "extra-judicial capacity", but what that meant in simple language was that they were ruthless killers who would use any violence necessary to suppress or eliminate enemies of white rule. Had their bosses ordered my murder? If so, would I be identified at the airport and dragged off in front of my family to a certain fate?

A thought suddenly struck me that I had not previously considered: what if I was arrested and hauled off to some place where I could be tortured at leisure to extract everything I knew about the operation of the ANC in my area, before my broken body was left on a roadside somewhere, as yet another warning to others like me? Violence was so endemic to our society that lynchings and torture were practiced almost as a matter of course by both opponents and supporters of apartheid, but the sudden horror of applying this possibility to myself caused me to break out in an intense sweat, and I slipped into the bathroom that led off our hotel suite so that Linda could not see my distress. I sat there on the edge of the bath, my head in my hands, and literally shook with fear.

How could I possibly summon the courage to walk up to the passport control officer tomorrow and calmly wait for him to pronounce my fate? Surely my panic would be noticeable? And what would happen to Linda and the children if I was taken away? They would be cast adrift in a hostile country, social pariahs with few resources to weather the storm of official condemnation that would surely break around them.

Perhaps we should call the whole thing off. If we simply drove back home tomorrow, nobody would be any the wiser about our intentions. Yet in the same instant I knew with an awful sense of finality that we could not go back; a bullet waited for me there. I was trapped at the end of a dark tunnel that led to a precipice and I saw no way out; there was no place to hide.

A devastating feeling of loneliness and despair washed over me and I suppressed the intense desire to cry out for help. Thoughts and emotions tumbled through my consciousness as I began to accuse myself for the folly of ever believing that I was somehow immune to punishment for choosing sides in the intensifying struggle for control of South Africa's future. I saw it so clearly now: the masses of people, both black and white, who sat mutely on the sidelines as the drama of South Africa's destiny unfolded were perhaps the only ones who ultimately would survive the power struggle unscathed. I had despised them for their lack of commitment, their passivity, but it seemed now that they would have the last laugh. I was a dead man, and few people would mourn my passing ten or twenty years from now, when instead of enjoying my golden years with my grandchildren I would lie moldering in some unkempt grave.

"Phillip, are you okay?"

Linda's worried voice through the bathroom door cut into my thoughts and I scrambled to draw my emotions together into a tight, controlled knot.

"Yes, I'm okay," I replied, my voice a hoarse croak. "I'll be out in a minute."

I stood and looked at myself in the bathroom mirror. Who was this stranger staring back at me; a man in his early forties with a weather-beaten face prematurely lined beneath a receding hairline? Did I really know this person? Did I understand the passions and the choices and the foibles that had brought me to this unhappy point in my life, or was I simply a victim of a cruel and immutable fate that had dealt me an indiscriminate hand from a rigged deck of cards? Did it really matter if I lived or died? Did anything I had accomplished in my life up to this moment really matter?

"No," I muttered in reply to myself, "it's all just a game!"

Strangely, this fatalistic bent in my thinking brought me sudden and unexpected strength. If this was all a game, then I was going to play it out as best I could. I might lose tomorrow, but fate would have to intervene and overrule my hard determination to get myself and my family safely through passport control and onto a plane and out of South Africa.

The calm that settled on me at this point stayed with me all through the night, giving me a restful sleep and allowing me to wake refreshed and energized, almost eager for the challenge that lay ahead.

Later that day we drove quickly to the airport and I deposited my car in the long-term parking area. If we failed either the first or second hurdle there was a faint possibility that we could come back to the car and perhaps make a very risky run for the Botswana border, 200 miles to the east. And if we never returned, anyone who claimed my car was welcome to it!

Then we were in the airport. Approaching the airline desk to check our bags and get our seat assignments, I felt a little like a condemned man walking his last mile. But I had set my mind like a steel trap and instead of causing me to fear this picture brought a thin smile to my lips. As our bags disappeared on a conveyor belt into the inner depths of the cargo area, where they would first be electronically screened and then sniffed by trained dogs seeking drugs or explosives, I bade them a silent prayer. I knew that some bags were randomly opened for more thorough searches and it was possible that a wide-awake security guard would wonder about four matching cans of talcum powder, but the chances of all of our bags being opened at once was remote, unless they were specially targeted. And then the game would be up anyway.

The challenge that lay immediately ahead dragged my mind away from this speculation. We stood now in a line that moved us first through a gate where our carry-on bags were screened, and then led us slowly but surely towards one of several booths where uniformed customs officials were checking passports. This was it!

As we came up to our booth I smiled at the impassive face that stared back at me, and placed our passports on the counter. The official reached out for them, and as he opened the first one I bent down and whispered into seven-year-old Lauren's ear, "Look, there's Mickey!"

Linda and I had primed the children at breakfast that morning, letting them know for the first time that we were on our way to Disneyland to see Mickey and Goofy and Tinker Belle and the rest of the cartoon gang. They were keyed up to a fever pitch of excitement, not understanding the idea of a long airplane ride and expecting at any moment to meet their idols through the next doorway or around the next corner. So when I told Lauren that Mickey was in view, she let out a shriek of anticipation and went running off down the drab corridor that led into the international lounge, calling "Mickey! Mickey! Mickey!"

"Hey, come back!" I yelled, and took off after her. I reached her in a few strides and grabbed her by the seat of her pants, then lifted her into my arms and walked back to the startled passport official. Smiling weakly at him, I explained, "We're going to Disneyland."

At the sound of the magic word, Lauren began squirming in my arms. Then, as if on cue, she started crying.

"Daddy, I want to see Mickey."

21

The official looked exasperated. "How long do you plan to be away?" he asked.

My adrenaline was pumping now and I was almost enjoying the game. Feigning similar exasperation, I looked half at Lauren and half at the man behind the counter and said, "Oh, we'll be back within two weeks. But, if these kids don't behave we may not go at all!"

At these dreaded words Lauren let out another wail. At Linda's side, nine-year-old Danielle also began to whimper. I felt a guilty twinge. Our children were normally well-behaved but Linda and I had deliberately revved them up for Mickey-sightings: there was a lot at stake in this fraught moment and I needed all the help I could get to distract the official's attention. It seemed to be working. I watched out of the corner of my eye as he paged rapidly through the passports. Then he began stamping each passport with an exit visa, and I wanted to shout with glee! But I suppressed the urge and instead said to the man, "You know, if they built Disneyland here we wouldn't have to go to all of this trouble and expense. I bet people would pay a lot to come here"

He nodded at me with a tight smile on his face as pushed the passports across the counter.

"Have a nice trip," he said, clearly believing that would be impossible with our two hyper-active Mickey-fanatics.

As we walked away from the booth Linda came up beside me and dug her fingers into my ribs.

"You're crazy," she whispered, "I nearly choked when you made that remark about building Disneyland here!"

She was referring to a private joke we shared with our friends: South Africa was such a very strange society that the country would outdraw Disneyland if they just built a wall around the place and charged admission!

"I'm sorry," I said. "The devil made me do it. I just couldn't resist a parting shot."

Then I chuckled with delight as I turned to her and added, "Do you realize we're through the worst part? Just a few more minutes and we'll be on that plane and out of here! In the meantime, let's focus on trying to get these poor children calmed down."

But the few minutes stretched to nearly two hours as we waited for our flight to be called, and the tension began to wear on me again. We were through passport control but until our plane was off the ground and out of South African airspace we were not yet entirely safe. Every time the public address system crackled to life I expected to hear our names called; every uniformed official who walked through the international lounge seemed to be heading straight for where we sat. I could tell the strain was affecting Linda too as she picked nervously at imaginary blemishes on her skirt. We attempted to make small talk but neither of us was interested in what the other had to say; we were each too wrapped up in our own thoughts and emotions. Thankfully, the children were calm, happily reading two of the comic books we had brought for them.

And then, suddenly, it was time to go. We gathered up our belongings and headed for the exit gate in response to the magical words announcing the departure of our flight. Within minutes we were entering the cool, brightly lit interior of the cavernous jumbo jet. Heading towards our seats, I studied the faces of the passengers around us, wondering what guilty secrets each of them was hiding, wondering which of them might be security agents, reminding myself for the thousandth time to guard my words and my behavior because we were not yet safe. But the anticipation of safety was becoming almost more than I could bear and as we settled into our seats I found myself willing the door to close and the huge aircraft to push away from the terminal. It was only when I saw an elderly man give me a strange look that I realized I was anxiously studying the face of everyone who entered, involuntarily seeking to identify the security policeman who would come and drag us back to captivity.

Then at last the door did close and we were moving across the apron, moving towards the runway, the four massive engines roaring now as we turned onto the takeoff path and were pushed back into our seats by the sudden rush of acceleration that propelled us down the two-mile long concrete strip and hurled us finally into the gathering night sky, the aircraft swooping sharply upwards and onwards and roaring and vibrating and thrusting away from the land that was our home but perhaps would never be seen by us again.

I realized I was squeezing Linda's hand but I could not speak as conflicting emotions crowded through me; exhilaration and loss and deep, deep sadness. I was suddenly aware that I was breaking a chord stretched back 323 years to the first of my European ancestors who had come to find their destiny in this land; could it be that as the last surviving member of my family to leave here, my going made their hardship and sacrifice and hope all in vain? Did I have any right to leave? Was it not my duty to die where they had died, mingling my blood with their blood that for centuries had soaked the soil of this place?

I groaned involuntarily with a painful sense of defeat, and Linda shot me a startled glance.

"It's okay," I said. "I'll be okay."

"Are we safe now?" asked Linda.

"Yes, honey, we're safe. We're free."

She was deep in thought for a moment, and then she suddenly blurted out: "So why don't I feel free? Oh, Phillip, I feel lost and lonely and afraid. Are you sure we're doing the right thing?"

I did not tell her that I was fighting my own doubts. But I could not pretend overwhelming confidence either, so instead I simply replied, "If staying alive is the right thing, and if creating an opportunity for our children to have a normal future to look forward to is the right thing, then, yes, absolutely, we're doing the right thing."

We both lapsed back into silence, and I forced myself to think about our next hurdle - admission to the United States. The Disneyland ploy had worked so well, masking my nervousness while distracting the South African passport officer, that I decided we would use the same approach at the other end.

Too soon for my frayed nerves to have recovered from the ordeal of getting out of South Africa, it was time for our moment of truth in America. The journey had taken 24 hours, including 16 hours of actual flying time and an eight-hour layover in Rio de Janeiro.

As we dragged ourselves off the plane, tired and disheveled, an alarm bell was sounding in my head.

"Don't blow it now," I told myself. "You're tired and impatient, but just take it easy."

A new fear had begun to grip me in the final hours of our approach to New York, our port of entry to the U.S. What if they didn't let us in? What then? What if they put us on a plane and sent us back to South Africa? The thought was too horrifying to dwell on; after risking so much and coming so far, surely they had to let us in! If they sent us back we'd be ruined.

I couldn't even bear to visualize the scene of our arrival back in Johannesburg, back to the tender care of a security police welcoming committee, back to their looks of angry triumph, back to despair and humiliation and, in my case, back to almost certain death.

"If there's a god in heaven, I sure hope he's looking out for us now," I said to myself as we made our way through the jostling crowds towards the Immigration and Naturalization officers who were the last barrier between us and freedom.

A friendly official took our passports and cast a practiced eye across our bedraggled little family.

"What brings you to the United States?" he asked innocently.

This was my cue. Despite their previous disappointment and the rigors of the long journey, the children had risen heroically to the call of Disneyland as Linda and I had encouraged them in the last hour that this really was it! We would soon be in that magical place called America, home of Disneyland! Soon, very soon, they would see Mickey and the gang.

So I gave the INS official my most winning smile and, pointing to the children, I said, "These two little things are on their way to Disneyland, and they're taking us with them!"

I marveled at the power of that fabled name as both Lauren and Danielle began to get excited again, vying for confirmation from Linda and I as they begged, "Are we really here? Can we go and see Mickey now? Can we? Can we?"

With a broad grin, the officer handed back our passports and spoke the sweetest words I had ever heard: "Well, it looks like you shouldn't disappoint them any longer. Welcome to the United States. Have a nice stay."

Almost in a trance, Linda and I took our first few steps into safety. We dared not look at each other, and did not speak, as we retrieved our suitcases and passed without incident through the customs area, then through the international gate into the main airport complex, then through the huge vaulted lobby and the massive glass doors and out into the sunlit street. All the way the tapping of our feet on the gleaming floors beat a rhythm that seemed to grow louder and more intense against the background noise and bustle of the jostling airport crowd, and the very air itself seemed to be charged with a strange electricity that finally enveloped us as we stood on the sidewalk and breathed the American outdoors for the first time: we were free!

We both knew it in the same instant.

We stopped, and turned, and smiled at each other, and reached eagerly for each other, and held tightly to each other. And then we wept.

CHAPTER TWO
A Small Event

"Mr. Thal, please answer the question!"

The slightly irritated voice of the government attorney cut into my thoughts and dragged my attention back to the present. Lost in my memories, I reluctantly forced my eyes to focus on the man staring at me, leaning forward a little at the waist, lips pursed, brow furrowed, a pencil drumming in the palm of one hand. Mid-thirties, somewhat bookish and neatly dressed in a buttoned-down sort of way, he looked every inch a lawyer with a very important train of questioning to pursue, but my daydreaming was slowing him down.

I looked across at the judge leaning back in his padded chair, an impassive, almost bored expression on his slightly older face. About my age, I guessed. Prematurely bald, like me. But that was about all we had in common. He did not acknowledge my glance, so I turned back to the lawyer. What was the question? Something about feelings, about the way I felt when I received the alleged phone call predicting my death. Yes, that was it: How did I feel when I heard the alleged threat? The lawyer's emphasis on the word alleged had not escaped my notice: in his view my whole fantastic story was an elaborate ploy designed to mislead the United States Government into granting me and my family unjustified asylum.

So he wanted me to describe my emotions, how I felt. He might as well have asked me to describe walking on the moon. Frustration gripped me as I looked around the drab courtroom. Linda and the children sat at a scuffed wooden table, with my lawyer at the far end. At an adjacent table was a team of three U.S. Immigration and Naturalization attorneys. Immediately to my right was the judge, seated on a raised podium. I had been told that this was not really a trial, more of a hearing, to determine my status. But it felt like a trial to me. It felt threatening and lonely to me.

Yes…that's how I felt: lonely. Perhaps a little afraid. But this government lawyer was not interested in the way I felt now: how had I felt then?

My sense of frustration threatened to overwhelm me. What could I possibly say in answer to such a question that would remotely convey the reality of my situation back in that strange, strange place so many miles away, so many worlds away, from this room in the U.S. Immigration and Naturalization regional headquarters in El Paso, Texas? It had been two years to the day since we fled South Africa but the passage of time and distance had not dulled the pain of our sudden departure, nor eased the nightmare implications of the fact that there, in my home, in the place of all my life and memories and hopes and dreams, a bullet waited for my return.

How could I hope to make it clear to those who were the happy beneficiaries of all the securities and protections of the United States Constitution, just what life was like in South Africa and what it felt like to be told that an assassin's bullet had your name on it? How could I make these solid, confident people understand my emotions, when all they knew from childhood was the certainty of their inalienable rights? They had never been afraid to call the police for help in a crisis, so what could I possibly say that would illustrate how it felt to experience the brittle tensions and anxieties of daily life in a country where police were the brutal enforcers of draconian legislation designed to keep nonconformists in line, and where those laws that did offer protection against the heavy hand of government were routinely manipulated in the most cynical fashion? Where were the words to describe such a thing, here, in this room, to a man from a different planet who wanted a ten-second answer?

Even as I wrestled with the impossibility of it all, my thoughts were suddenly drawn back to a South African courtroom where my sense of helplessness and despairing frustration was startlingly similar to the way I felt now. But this American lawyer was not going to let me go there.

"Mr. Thal! Please!" he barked.

I stared helplessly back at him. My mouth was dry. I needed time to think.

"Could I..." my voice croaked, "...could I have a glass of water?"

The lawyer grimaced. With a brief nod he indicated the water jug on the table in front of Linda. She brought a glass across to me and as I sipped the cool liquid I saw in my minds eye a vivid picture of that other courtroom.

I remembered a fat blue-fly buzzing furiously against a windowpane, determined to bore its way to freedom from the stifling confines of the large room. It was very hot, mid-summer in Johannesburg. Large double doors stood open to a blasting sun that drove all coolness from the porch and bounced heat waves across to where I sat alone, having arrived early in court to contest a speeding fine.

To the casual glance I might have appeared to be asleep. But behind my shuttered eyelids I was imagining cool sensations as a last defense against the suffocating heat, until a small sound intruded on my thoughts and I opened my eyes to see that two traffic clerks had entered the courtroom and were arranging stacks of yellow files on the long brown table that stood below the magistrate's raised throne.

I closed my heavy eyes again. Perhaps if I imagined hard enough I could return to a place of cool breezes and gently singing waterfalls. But a new sound pegged me firmly in the present time and space. Through the lashes of my barely open eyes I watched a stout policeman climb the last of the stairs from the holding cells below into the accused's dock that stood in the center of the courtroom. In his wake came a reluctant stumbling figure, his steps made awkward by the handcuffs that joined him to the policeman.

They entered the dock. Here the policeman slipped the handcuff off his wrist and clapped it on the vacant wrist of his companion. Than he stepped out of the dock through the small swing gate at the top of the stairs, barely glancing at me as he passed by.

"Now let's see some justice!" the policeman bellowed, jarring me from my slump and causing me to focus fully on the scene before me.

The man in the dock looked to be about middle age. Slightly built and neatly dressed. Too neat, if your skin was black and you wanted to avoid undue attention from the police. Perhaps this black man knew

31

no better. Or thought he was smart enough to avoid trouble.

The policeman subscribed to the latter view. Placing himself squarely in front of his quarry he stood with straddled legs and hands on hips and said as much: "So, you think you're very clever, don't you, my friend? Very clever. But I caught you anyway. Yes I did! And now do you know what you're going to do?"

The question hung menacingly in the air between them as the policeman rocked back on his heels and took a long look down his nose at his prisoner in the dock. The man said nothing, hanging his head and averting his gaze, the acceptable procedure for acknowledging the wisdom and power of white authority. But the policeman wanted a response.

Raising his voice he demanded, "Do you know what you're going to do?"

The man said nothing.

"Look at me when I talk to you," the policeman demanded. "Look at me, you black bastard!"

With that he lunged forward and grabbed the man by his shirt, dragging him against the railing of the dock. Their faces inches apart, the policeman yelled: "Do you know what you're going to do? You're going to plead guilty! Yes, that's right. Guilty! When the judge comes in here I want no nonsense from you. Now show me how you're going to say it, you rude black bastard."

The black man staggered as his shirtfront was released. He gazed dumbly at his tormentor, working a well-rehearsed passive blankness into every corner of his face so that not the slightest hint of resistance showed to feed the frenzy of hatred confronting him. But the policeman was determined.

"Say it! Let me hear you say it! I'm guilty! Guilty! Guilty!"

No response.

The policeman looked nonplused for a moment. Then a cunning expression crossed his reddened face as a new thought occurred to him.

"Let me show you the way it's going to be," he smiled softly. "You're going to raise your right hand in the dock and swear to tell the truth. You are going to stand there in front of the judge and raise your right hand. Yes you are."

The policeman raised his right hand in demonstration.

"Now show me how you raise your hand."

With a desperate look on his face the man in the dock mutely held his wrists away from his body, indicating that he could not raise his right hand because it was cuffed to his left. But this small response was a mistake, giving the policeman the opening he was looking for, and he pounced on it.

"That's okay," he said softly, like a cat playing with a mouse. "This is only for practice. You can raise both hands above your head."

Slowly, warily, the prisoner did as he was told. As his elbows reached waist height, cuffed wrists just below his chin, the policeman hit him.

It was an extraordinarily hard blow delivered with surprising speed as the big man lunged forward to take full advantage of the small target offered to his practiced fist. He caught the prisoner directly in the solar plexus and drove him back against the rear wall of the dock where he crashed and bounced and slid in agony to his knees, then tumbled slowly to his side.

The policeman placed both hands on the dock and peered inside to watch his victim writhe and cough and gasp for air.

"Hey, now don't put on such an act," he said in a friendly tone. "I didn't hit you that hard. Come on now, stand up."

But the man stayed down.

"Damn! I don't know when last I met one as stubborn as you," the policeman spat disgustedly. "Stand up, you fool. Or must I make you stand up?"

He came around the side of the dock and entered through the swing gate. The man still lay gasping. There was a soft thud as the policeman sank his boot into yielding flesh. Then he bent and grabbed what his hands could find and yanked the man to unsure feet.

"Are you going to plead guilty?"

No reply.

The man was lifted easily into the air and shaken like a rag doll. Then dropped. He fell awkwardly and scrabbled to his knees, finding himself at the top of the stairs leading to the cells below.

The policeman came up behind and kicked him. With a strangled groan the man plunged head-first down the stairs, closely followed by the thudding of heavy boots and a booming voice that accused him, between blows, of stubbornness or trying to escape. Then silence.

In the courtroom the fat blue-fly buzzed and two traffic clerks made lazy conversation at the table.

I blinked. I had not moved in the 90 seconds it had taken for the brutal little drama to unfold. No one else, nothing else, had moved. The two main actors might have been invisible for all the distraction their confrontation caused in this quiet, stifling courtroom.

Perhaps I was asleep. I wished I was asleep, and this was all a dream. The implications of the shocking, violent spectacle disturbed me so deeply I felt ill. It had been so swift, yet casual, so entirely commonplace as not even to disturb the two officials in their idle chatter. Surely, it must be a dream. I closed my eyes. And opened them. And wondered what to do.

I should report the incident. But to whom? To the police? My bitter laugh made a hollow sound in the back of my throat. Then I stared at the court officials. They were the obvious ones to remedy this situation. I rose slowly to my feet and walked across to the table where they sat. Stopping between them, I looked first at the one, and then the other. Blank stares met me in return. Pointing back at the dock, I asked a rhetorical question:

"You saw that?"

One man, the older of the two, narrowed his eyes and spat a blunt reply: "What?"

"That. That back there. The policeman."

The man turned to his companion. "What's he talking about?"

"I dunno."

Then to me, "No, man, you must be dreaming."

With that, they both turned their backs on me and continued their interrupted conversation. The insult was deliberate, brazen. I stared at them for a moment, wondering if I should challenge them again. Then I turned and walked from the courtroom, anger boiling inside me. Outside, in the oppressive heat, I saw a payphone near the entrance to the Magistrate's Court and walked over to it. A quick search of the telephone directory produced the number for The Star, Johannesburg's big daily newspaper. Within seconds I was speaking to the news desk.

The voice on the other end of the line was jaded and impatient in response to my telling of the events I had just witnessed.

"We appreciate you calling, sir, but I don't think we can run this story."

"Why not?" I protested.

There was a long pause, and then the voice said very deliberately, "Because your story is full of emotion and we're supposed to report only the facts..."

I cut in to underline what I thought was obvious: "Those are the facts. It all happened right in front of me!"

"Sir, listen to me," the voice responded, exasperation evident in its tone, "the only fact here is that you claim to have seen it happen. That's all. You got nothing else. Not the name of the policeman. Not his number. No name for the victim. You don't even have names for the two traffic clerks who were with you in the courtroom. And on top of all that, I have absolutely no idea who you are."

"No, you listen to me!" I responded angrily. "What happened in that courtroom was terrible. I'll come to your office immediately and identify myself and tell you the whole story face to face. I may not have all the facts but I'm an eyewitness. Surely that's enough!"

"No, sir, that's not enough. Your word alone is just not good enough. I appreciate your concern, but if we run this story the police will not only come after us, they'll come after you, also; and unless you're very tough, they'll break you like a twig."

I felt my stomach churn as I replied with a bravado I did not really feel: "It's a risk I'm prepared to take."

"Maybe. But we're not," the voice shot back. Then, in a softer tone, the man said, "Look, sir, I know how upsetting this must be for you. And I don't doubt that you're telling the truth. But if you'll just step back from your emotions for a moment, I think you'll agree with me that not very much happened there. It's not worth putting your neck on the line for this relatively *minor event*."

"A what?" I asked, incredulous. "What did you call it?"

With a note of finality that indicated our conversation was over, the voice repeated, "It's tragic, I know; but at the end of the day it's really no big deal. Just a small event…"

+++++++++++++++++++

Now here I was in another courtroom, in another place, and although the circumstances were very different my disbelieving ears were hearing the same words again. Startled, I focused on the earnest face of the government lawyer confronting me, and I watched intently as his mouth formed the words he was repeating.

"Mr. Thal, let me say it again: You're having difficulty describing your emotions in response to the alleged death threat against you because it really was a small event, just a single event, and you want to make us believe that it was enough to cause you to run for your life. Isn't that really what's happening here, Mr. Thal?"

The sudden emotion released within me by the hearing of that jarring phrase caused me to reply with a passion I had not previously felt. I had been slouched in my chair, but now I straightened up and leaned towards my interrogator.

"No! That's not what's happening here," I said firmly. "And your choice of words is most unfortunate. In South Africa, small events were associated with children's birthdays and minor league tennis, but there was never anything minor about events in the political arena. It was all big time. They were all big issues. Life or death issues. You can't understand that because to you the Vietnam War protests or the Watts riots were a big deal, and they were, in the American context. But compared to what happened almost daily in South Africa, especially in the 80s and early 90s, especially in the black townships where kids confronting armed troops threw their lives away like so much dirty laundry, your upheavals were nothing much.

"What we're dealing with here is a vast difference in perceptions about the way things were and the possibilities that existed for real personal harm. It wasn't a small event when Nelson Mandela was hauled off to jail for 27 years. It wasn't a small event when Steve Biko was tortured and beaten to death in police custody. It wasn't a small event when police at Sharpeville shot scores of protesting women and children in the back. And it wasn't a small event when I led a protest march through the streets of my home town behind a truck filled with policemen holding their fingers on the triggers of automatic rifles, every one of them pointed straight at me, and the images of a dozen Sharpevilles vivid in my mind. It wasn't a small event when my friend was shot in the back of the head. It wasn't a small event when a molotov cocktail was thrown at my house...

"...and, no, sir, in the context of so much everyday cruelty and hatred and violence and bloodshed, it didn't at all seem a small event the night a onetime friend of mine called to warn me that a hit squad had selected me as their next target for assassination!"

I paused, a little winded by my outburst, and looked around the room. Taking a deep breath, I was about to continue when the judge gave a polite cough and said quietly, "I think we need to take a ten-minute recess."

CHAPTER THREE
Separation

I touched the soul of Africa once, on a farm in the southeastern lowlands.

Wildlife roamed free there. One evening a group of visitors rode down a bumpy trail on the back of an open truck into the last of the setting sun. The air was warm and still and the untamed veld was alive with birdcalls and the furtive shufflings of animals seeking shelter for the night, or predators rousing for the hunt. We drove for about an hour while darkness gathered, catching glimpses of wildebeest and zebra and giraffes and the occasional majestic kudu and ubiquitous impala and warthogs scurrying away with erect thin tails like radio antennae. The feeling was one of being an intruder. Browsing animals disdained even to spare us a glance as we drove slowly by.

Soon there was a full moon riding into the deepening black vault of the sky and its pale luminescence gave a haunting quality to the unfamiliar terrain that pressed on us from every side. I moved back and knelt at the tailgate of the truck to watch the slow unfolding of the sandy path beneath us as we idled down a shallow incline towards a stand of dense low trees. No one spoke. Among the trees, soft shapes in the moonlight and shadow, browsed impala. I bent my head to stare at them for a moment before turning my gaze back to the path.

Then the breath froze in my lungs and sweat prickled every pore in my body. Literally inches from my disbelieving eyes was the face of a lioness. I wanted to cry out but the strength drained from me. I wanted to hide but there was nowhere to go. I crouched, transfixed like a cornered animal, watching her; the massive yellow features, the short rounded ears with their tufts of white hair, the wide, blunt nose, and the pale-gold expressionless eyes with no depth to them and no connection to a soul or to a germ of compassion. It was the face of death.

She moved at the same slow pace as the truck, gliding softly across the sand, relaxed yet immensely purposeful in the way her head hung low against her shoulders. I waited breathless for her to take me, until she gave a furtive glance towards the trees. Then with a gut-churning flood of relief my fear turned to fascination, as I understood that the lioness was not stalking me but the impala, using the vehicle as cover. She hardly seemed aware of me, but followed so close for a full minute that I could hear her soft panting and feel the enormous power radiating from the silken weight of her deliberate step. Every facet of her was exquisitely aligned to her hunter's purpose, tensing like a bowstring in the second before the arrow flies. She was all grace and perfect killing instinct.

That instinct drove her now as her huge muscled frame began to coil, easing lower to the ground. Her nose jutted forward. Then she lifted her head and in a single lithe bound plunged into the trees. The impala responded as if a switch had been thrown. Instant startled forms flashed in unison through the scattered moonlight; twisting, stretching, bunching, weaving, dashing as each chose an instinctive path away from the death that pursued them with such eager furious energy. For a frantic moment the trees were a maelstrom. And then just as suddenly it was quiet again.

Miraculously, the entire herd escaped in the confusion, aided by their numbers and the thick brush, despite the emergence of a second lioness from the shadows at the corner of the wood where she had been lying in ambush. The incredible burst of activity was over so quickly that some of those in the back of the truck saw nothing. They had been looking in the wrong direction when the attack came.

To the right of us, across from the trees, an open meadow unfolded into a small grassy depression with a pool of water at its center. A single twisted tree stood at the water's edge. The lionesses emerged into this meadow after a minute or two, accompanied by their larger black-maned mate. As the three made their leisurely way down to the water the languid droop of their heads and tails and the relaxed fluid motions of their bodies radiated power and dominance. They feared nothing here. There was no need to be alert. They simply walked straight to the water, crouched side by side, and began to drink. Overhead the fat yellow moon hung lazy on a dense black field pricked by spangled stars as bright as diamonds.

The world stopped turning. Time was suspended. I could scarcely breathe for the beauty of it, the perfection of it: soft light and warm air soft against my cheek; a low night chorus of insects all around; gentle sounds of small things moving through the grass; and at the focal point a gnarled tree and huddled lions duplicated in absolute symmetry from the shallow depths of the reflective pool. It was a mystical tableau, ancient as the world itself, etched forever on the night.

And on my grateful memory.

It is said that if the red soil of Africa gets into your blood you will always be drawn back to her bosom. Now as I sat in a strange land so far from Africa's embrace the haunting quality of that introduction to her primeval heart was vivid with me still, underscoring the pain of separation.

Nothing about coming to America had been easy or pleasant. The frightening circumstances of our hurried departure from home, the desperate tension at the airport, the awful feeling of dismemberment as the giant aircraft wrenched itself free from the earth, the tedious flight, and then the entrance into America itself all had the quality of a nightmare.

Exhausted from the long journey, we spent the night at a hotel near Kennedy Airport before flying on to Albuquerque. There, my brother met us and took us to our new temporary home, a partly furnished two-bedroom apartment. The stricken look on Linda's face as we walked through the door spoke volumes for her state of mind. But she held her emotions in check until later that night, when she clung to me as we lay in bed and her tears washed my shoulder.

This tiny place, so small and mean after the comfortable spaciousness of the house we had shared for many years, would be our home for the foreseeable future. The sudden change in our circumstances was profound. Until a few days ago - centuries ago now, it seemed - we had lived the lifestyle, if not of the famous, then certainly of the rich. Our wealth had never been anything that we flaunted but it did buy us much in the way of ease and comfort and entertainment that we had come to take almost for granted. Now we would have to count every penny of our limited funds to make the dollars stretch; for how long?

I thought back with something approaching nostalgia to the indolent early days of our marriage, when life was easy and politics had not yet become my ruling passion. In those days, the mid- to late-70's, life in South Africa was near perfect if you were young and white and upwardly mobile. There seemed to be no limit to where ambition could take you, with the economy booming from a high gold price and relative peace in the land. Peace was always relative, never absolute, because of the intractable issues raised by the fact that a small, privileged minority ruled a large deprived majority, but for a time when our primary focus was the party scene and establishing a money-making career, South Africa seemed the best place in the world to be and people like our rich friends the Chandlers were our role models.

Marty and Susan Chandler seemed to live for the weekends. "People like us," they would say, "like to relax, let our hair down, on weekends."

People like them were forty-something, affluent, confident, and comfortable in their designer home with swimming pool and tennis court tucked behind high stone walls. People like them worked hard; Marty as a company director, Susan at charitable activities or meeting girlfriends in fashionable cafes for tea, playing bridge, tanning beside the pool, planning dinner parties, directing work on her sprawling garden. Sometimes dallying with a small affair. It was all hard work.

Friday nights were dinner times at home, theirs or a friend's; formal sit-down do's with six or eight couples, four course meals and the best French wines. Conversations revolved mostly around business and politics, mostly politics, although the best hostesses ensured through a clever mix of old and new friends that the talk also veered to more esoteric subjects. Wives would sometimes discuss problem servants.

Saturdays were devoted to shopping and golf or tennis. The nights brought forays with friends to the theatre or dancing at the club or dining at the newest restaurant.

Conversations were dominated by business or politics. Wives sometimes discussed their problem servants.

On Sunday Marty and Susan liked to wake late and enjoy breakfast in bed served by Ellen, who seldom showed the strain of her 12-hour days as cook, cleaner, server, launderer, pet-minder and surrogate mother to three small children. Ellen, to the envy of Susan's friends, was not a problem servant. She did not steal, did not drink, never entertained men in her tiny room secreted behind the double garage and only occasionally complained about the rigors of her job. She was a rare jewel, Susan was proud to say.

Sunday began in earnest when breakfast was done and the papers were read and the family had splashed together in the pool to wash away the jaded edges of the week gone by, while Ellen made up the bedrooms and ensured that the house was spotlessly clean. Then Susan and Ellen prepared for the traditional open house by spreading a table under the awning on the patio beside the pool; beer and wine and champagne on ice and little delicacies and the second best silver and crystal. Friends would start to arrive at about noon, perhaps a little later, to stay for an hour or two before moving on to the next party, or to prepare to host their own sundowners.

The Chandler open house was highly rated for the fact that the food and drink were inexhaustible and the party never closed 'til late, sometimes as late as midnight. There was a constant coming and going of friends, with some cheerful souls staying the entire course and playing temporary hosts when Marty and Susan took their short afternoon nap.

Conversation was dominated by business and politics. Wives discussed their problem servants.

Problem servants and problem politics were really two sides of the same coin, a black coin that perplexed and frustrated the Chandlers and their friends. It was a problem that would not go away, persistently intruding on every waking moment and robbing them of complete enjoyment of their rich and sunny lifestyle. There were just so many blacks; it was impossible to ignore them and their multitude of needs and wants. Equally, it was impossible to live without them because their abundant and cheap unskilled labor was what helped to make life so rich and sunny.

So we would get together for our weekend parties and I would listen in fascination as Marty and his rich friends tried to square the political circle. Clearly, some of them believed apartheid was wrong. As were some of the government's wilder actions in suppressing opposition when it seemed to go too far. But, on the other hand, experience elsewhere in Africa had shown that black governments were just as brutal and were equally unable to bring peace to their troubled lands.

Marty was particularly strident in his expressions of opposition to the apartheid system and his friends accused him of spending too much time overseas on business, where he was forced to listen to the views of people who did not understand South Africa's complexity. George, Marty's best friend, thought so. George could not understand why Marty wasted so much time agonizing about the injustices of apartheid. Life in South Africa was the best in the world, George often reminded him. Moreover, the country's blacks were better off than anywhere else in Africa.

"Sure," George would concede, "some things are wrong here, but what country's perfect? America doesn't treat its blacks any better; they're just more devious about it. Our only problem is that we're honest; we have an official policy that lets our blacks know exactly where they stand. And let's face it, most of them are too damn ignorant to know what's good for them. Without white brains and technology this country would be nothing."

I watched Marty squirm when George spoke this way. His friend made no secret of the fact that he was a government supporter, something rarely encountered in Marty's circle, although it seemed to me that those others of his friends who adopted a superior attitude towards George because of his unfashionable stance were themselves so effete in their opposition to apartheid as to make their views meaningless. Privately, I despised them for their weak-kneed self-indulgence, although my own views had not yet crystallized to the point where I felt I could express them with confidence.

As I lay there in that strange Albuquerque bed and relived those far-off experiences I sought to trace the genesis of my alienation from the common perspective on life in South Africa's white paradise. Much of it lay in my naturally rebellious spirit that reacted with increasing disdain against the dead hand of authority whose weight permeated all of our existence, from the regimentation of schooldays to the solemn patriotism drummed into us during our compulsory military service and seemingly demanded of us forever after by a ruling establishment that saw itself increasingly at odds with world opinion. Yet it was clear to me that much of the conflict with the rest of the world came from the establishment's matchless propensity for bizarre pronouncements and idiotic actions fuelled largely by its smug belief that it ruled by divine right.

To my mind, daily life in South Africa was a bit like being in the boarding school to which I had been sent at a very young age. The peculiar British habit of getting rid of your children as soon as decency permits, by sending them away to be cared for by strangers, had been exported to the colonies with much else of inappropriate British culture and it was in such a place that the foundation of my cynicism and disillusionment was laid.

The school was a fitting metaphor for all that was dysfunctional about our society and its government.

Named after a remote queen who had absolutely nothing in common with our lives, it attempted to ape the more exclusive British institutions with grim stone and ivy-covered walls and Masters who wore somber black gowns and boys who dressed in very proper uniforms topped by Henley-type straw hats called "boaters" or "cheese-cutters". Beyond these outward trappings it was an austere, brutal environment; a place where small boys were cast adrift by well-meaning or uncaring parents to be terrorized and victimized by bigger boys who were terrorized and victimized by those who were bigger still, all of them victims of a system where the highest virtue was discipline strictly enforced. There was no love there, no compassion, no place to seek comfort or to expose weaknesses. Weakness attracted darts and assaults as numerous and as hateful as flies swarming on a corpse, so the good sense of the admonition to keep a stiff upper lip was quickly learned as a fundamental requisite for survival. Boys turned inwards for their strength and expended much of their energy in weaving outer garments of cynicism and self-sufficiency.

The school itself was an intellectual wasteland. The teachers who populated it were for the most part men of small achievement and large egos who thrived in a closed environment where their incompetence was never tested because their word could not be questioned. Others were heartbroken idealists whose rage and bitterness at submitting to the charade was vented on the young minds they once dreamed of inspiring. Either way, we the unknowing, taught by the unfeeling or the unwilling, were sacrificed daily on the altar of mindless conformity to a myth of what it meant to be white and a ruler of the universe.

It was an exquisite irony that in this place whose pompous exterior so venerated the god of learning, the highest achievement year after year was to produce a new batch of disciplined clods. By the time I was fourteen the grotesque system had effectively destroyed any desire I might have had to become educated.

But an unintended consequence of the institutionalized alienation provided some treasured diversions that also played an important role in molding the values that would inspire my destiny. Lonely white boys like myself sometimes turned for friendship and for comfort to the only sympathetic human beings we could find; the black janitors who existed almost invisibly on the fringes of school life.

Jim was the name of the janitor at our hostel. It was not his real name, a fact that I discovered one evening as we sat and smoked a pipe together, but he answered quite cheerfully to Jim because it was a convenient handle for his white masters. He was special: old and wise and very kind, with a gracious courtly manner that would not permit him to register shock or displeasure at the aberrant behavior he saw each day around him in the strange world of the school. Often he played host outside his tiny room to a gathering of small boys for whom his doorstep was neutral territory and his smile of greeting a sought-for antidote to the petty, painful events of another traumatic day.

I could not recall a single intellectual highlight from all those long wasted years at school. But I vividly remembered Jim's warm smile and the stories he told of Africa. He spoke with a deep fondness and pride of his land and of the rich heritage and history of his people, who lived in a magical-sounding place across the Kei River. There, young boys played all day among the herds of cattle that they tended, and at night they sat close around the hearth fires listening to elders tell the stories from the past. Jim was a Xhosa, a nation who had once been stronger and more numerous than the mighty Zulu and who had first borne the brunt of the white man's entrance into Southern Africa. The Xhosa might have prevailed against the whites but for a tokoloshe, an evil spirit, who appeared in a vision to a young girl and instructed her that if the people killed all their cattle and burnt all their crops, a great wind would come and sweep the whites into the sea.

Instead it was the Xhosa, weakened by starvation and disheartened by the failure of the prophecy, who were swept aside. Jim made sure we understood the moral of the story. "You see, my little masters, it is important for you to work hard in school and learn all you can," he would tell us gravely, "because then you will be wise to know when an evil spirit tells you lies."

It was incomprehensible to Jim that we did not view our schooling as a rare and privileged opportunity to advance ourselves in life. He reacted with anger or distress when we sat in his company and complained among ourselves about the shortcomings and injustices of the school system and he would admonish us again and again to never stop learning.

Jim never spoke of how he came to be in this place, but the wounds and bitter memories he bore showed sometimes in his pained expression as he remembered how a great and proud warrior nation had been reduced to waiting on the white man's pleasure. He felt a special shame for his lack of formal education, although he was no different from most others of his race who were subject to an official policy that stated without self-consciousness or hint of any apology that

51

for the good of the white ruling class, and their own good, blacks should not be educated beyond the status of hewers of wood and drawers of water.

Yet for all the injustices and slights that he suffered daily, almost as a matter of course, I saw Jim truly angry at white authority only once. The experience left an indelible impression on me as I witnessed him being reprimanded by the hostel master for failing to respond quickly enough to an order. The man was young and white and arrogant, supremely confident and careless in his status, and all he saw before him was a bowed and gray-haired kaffir too stupid or too lazy to follow his instructions. My heart ached for my comforter and friend as I watched the cruel words lash him, more painful than any whip.

Later that day I tried to commiserate with Jim, but with a curt wave of his hand he cut me short. We sat in silence for a time as I realized that my friend was trying to compose himself, to control the anger that boiled inside him.

"What that kwedien - that little boy - did, was not right," Jim said at last, his voice harsh and bitter.

I was shocked to hear him use such a disparaging term about a white master and I could only wonder at the depth of the wound that Jim felt. But his next words left me mortified.

"I'm sorry, my little master. I'm sorry he did that in front of you. He should not have done such a thing."

Jim's concern was not for himself, but for me, for the ugliness that I had witnessed. I was stunned that this gracious old man wanted somehow to shield me from the brutal reality of his life, and it was several minutes before I could speak. Then as I looked at him through the tears that filled my eyes I made him a solemn vow: "I am sorry, too. And one day, I promise you, one day I will make this thing right."

Jim smiled. "One day the great N'kosi will make everything right."

Then, as he so often did, Jim went on to tell me a story that had a wonderful moral attached to it.

When God first made man, Jim recounted, he formed man from the rich black clay of the river bank; the same clay that children use to this day to fashion abundant herds of sleek hump-backed oxen. Not surprisingly, the first man was black, and so were his two brothers whom God later made to keep him company. They were all three very beautiful, but it was impossible to tell them apart. So God made a magical pool of water and told the second brother to swim there. When he did, the blackness washed away and left him pale and white. The third brother was also instructed to wash, but when he left the now muddy water he was a pale brown color. And so the three different races of men were formed.

"But God always loved the black man most, because he was the first son," Jim explained. "That is why some white men hate us now. They are jealous."

Then, with a distant look in his eyes, Jim softly concluded: "On the other side of life, where God's home is, black people sit around his fire and it is the whites who serve them. I do not mean to be unkind when I say this, little master, but I think I will like that place."

I took the opportunity to tell Jim he should stop calling me klein basie - little master.

"No! No!" he replied, smiling kindly. "I must call you this. You are my friend, but you are white, and you are my master. If I stop calling my white friend my master, then one day I will forget to call somebody my master, who is not my friend, and then he will be very angry with me like that kwedien was a while ago."

I could not refute Jim's logic so I left the matter there. But many years later my vow to him to "make things right" began to mature as with increasing vehemence I voiced my disillusionment with South Africa. I had heard all the hackneyed old arguments a thousand times from people like Marty and his friends and as I developed and articulated my own position, which questioned much of the conventional wisdom, my younger circle of friends began to view me as something of a liberal. In the South African context this was akin to wearing a bell around your neck and carrying a sign that declared, "Unclean!"

I put myself wholly beyond the pale when I toyed with the unthinkable suggestion that the ultimate solution to our country's problems might be one-man-one-vote. This viewpoint invariably caused debate so heated that Linda and I were invited to some parties for the spice I might add. We were excluded forever from others for precisely the same reason.

For me the issue was clear-cut: apartheid was wrong. Yet, as with so much else in South Africa, the solution was not nearly as neatly definable as the problem and I was not entirely sure that a fully representative democracy would indeed provide the answer. There were so many different tribal factions that I doubted any government - black or white - could rule without a measure of force and some exclusion of opposition interests. Even the white "tribe" itself was divided between Afrikaans-speakers - those of mainly Dutch descent who generally supported the ruling party - and English-speakers, who stridently opposed the government but privately seemed grateful that somebody else was doing the dirty work of keeping blacks subservient to white rule. In addition to these two factions, there were eight or nine clearly definable black groups divided mainly along the lines of tribe, culture and language.

A major explanation of how so few whites could subdue and rule so many blacks lay in the fact that the minority white regime had done a masterful job of balkanizing the country through its "homelands" policy, raising the concept of "divide and rule" to an art form by splitting and isolating the different interest groups into hostile camps who fought each other as much as they fought the government. South Africa's official slogan - "Unity Is Strength" -was laughably cynical because there were probably few societies on earth as fractured as this one!

So when it came time to choose sides in the struggle the issue was a little more complicated than black v. white. For one thing, most active resistance to apartheid - as opposed to mere posturing - was led by liberals whom I disliked for their infuriating superior attitudes, or by their socialist and Marxist cousins for whom I also had a strong antipathy, sharing Nietzche's view that socialism represented the tyranny of the least and the dumbest.

Yet I had found in Nietzsche another thought that exactly described the form of South Africa's tragedy, pointing ominously to its fate and fuelling my own private inner torments until at last I threw in my lot with the Marxist-supported African National Congress. Nietzsche argued that it is the experience of being powerless that ultimately releases the most destructive forces in men.

"Nihilism is a symptom," he said, "that the underprivileged have no comfort left; that they destroy in order to be destroyed; that without morality they no longer have any reason to resign themselves - that they place themselves on the plane of opposite principle and also want power by compelling the powerful to become their hangmen."

This stark warning was confirmed daily in the escalating violence that erupted like a suppurating boil on South Africa's sunny face. Inevitably, that violence would sweep me up in its bloodstained arms.

CHAPTER FOUR
Innocence

Before the brutalizing school years, before adulthood and politics, before violence and bloodshed, there was innocence.

I remember how we trekked along the rugged coast of south-east Africa by covered wagon; ten days of walking and riding behind a team of sixteen solid, stolidly plodding oxen with fierce white horns and gleaming hides the color of the rich red African earth that paved our way. The wagon was huge. A rumbling, creaking, awesome construction of weather-worn oak and coarse black beaten steel topped by a faded and ratty white canopy that swayed and swatted and billowed to the motion of the wagon and the tugging of the wind.

It did not seem a very special adventure, then. Covered wagons were rare, even in 50's Africa, and trekking in one was rarer still, but I did not know that. We were on vacation, a special event organized by a group of farming friends who were all descended from pioneering stock, but to my very young awareness the experience seemed no more worthy of note than others that caused me to skip and laugh through the carefree apple-green days.

Many years later I learned that the covered wagon had been rebuilt partly from the remains of one that carried the hopes and small possessions of a family of white pioneers into Africa's dark heartland almost a century before, and I was moved to reflect on the fact that perhaps some spirit from those times touched me as I slept each night on the wagon's weathered boards.

How else could I explain that so often, when innocence was all gone, I felt like a stranger in this strange compelling land?

But back then, before the disturbing sense of alienation gripped my soul, my corner of Africa was a magical place. Basotholand (now the independent Kingdom of Lesotho) was a tiny British protectorate in the heart of South Africa. It was sometimes likened to Switzerland, although the similarity extended only to the fact that it was small and entirely mountainous. For the rest, this rugged home of a million blanket-clad tribes people was a primitive backwater. Roads catered more to horses, the principal means of transportation, and to livestock, the principal basis of commerce, than to wheeled vehicles. Telephones were a rarity, so that most long-distance communication was by short-wave radio. And electricity, if you had it, was provided by loudly thudding two-stroke generators that coughed oily black smoke and powered a few feeble, flickering lightbulbs in the spartan homes of relatively affluent white traders.

The dozens of trading stations that dotted the mountains and valleys of the tiny country provided very modest points of contact with modern European styles and values. In some subtle ways the personality of each station varied under the influence of the tough husband and wife teams who ran them, but in outline they were generally all the same.

Each was a magnet that drew their small surrounding world to them along a skein of paths and tracks and rutted roads that daily channeled an ambling ebb and flow of myriad bright blankets. Here along a path you might see a maroon and pink and white and brown dazzle in the shape of a mother surrounded by excited squealing children. There a smudge of dignified, somber colors wrapped around a group of solemn-faced matrons, moving like a pantomime of galleons in full sail. To one side a feather of dust marks the progress of a donkey-sled piled high with sheepskins for trade, tended by a startling mash of multi-colored swirls and flashes from which emerges a grizzled face topped by a bright stocking cap.

On another path a young rebel throws aside the ubiquitous blanket to show of his new city suit; a statement made more emphatic by the absence of shirt and shoes. Elsewhere a family group looks like a neatly tended flowerbed in their matching blankets and red bonnets. And flowing with the tide, yet aloof, blanket-covered men sit loftily on horseback, moving singly or in pairs, some accompanied by their wives who walk a respectful ten paces behind, perhaps carrying the day's shopping on their heads. The women step with a special grace, their balance and concentration causing each one to wear her load like a queen with a crown.

As the paths converge on the trading station they become better defined, broadening from their many linking tributaries, now wide enough to carry the occasional dust-riddled bus or battered truck. Trees appear, mostly tall green-drab bluegums that offer little shade but serve to outline the boundaries of the low-slung ramble of stone and corrugated iron buildings that marks the center of the station. The crowd funnels towards it. At the entrance to the store itself, through the dusty courtyard with its sentinels of giant prickly pear trees, horses stand sway-backed at a hitching post.

A shallow flight of weathered stone steps leads to a porch running the length of the building. The porch is cluttered with bales of wool and farming implements and children scampering and men smoking contemplative pipes as they wait for their bales to be weighed on the big black scales standing at one corner. At the center of all the bustle stands a doorway, the ultimate promise of reward.

Modern doorways are merely holes that lead nowhere special, anemic portals to a sterile conformity that promises nothing. But at a trading station that is the center of its own universe, the doorway is a sensual introduction to a heady mix of sights and sounds and smells and tastes and touches that leave you drunk with sensations and link you to another world whose dimensions are only dreamed of - the twentieth century that gleams, always hidden but strongly rumored, somewhere beyond the furthest horizon.

This inviting entrance is always large and cool and dim, etched in sharp contrast to the harsh bright sunshine blasting everything outdoors. As you enter your eyes take a moment to adjust to the pale light that filters through a few small flyspecked windows and flickers from an occasional candle or old brass lamp. Under you the worn and dusty floorboards are polished smooth and soft by the passage of untold numbers of shuffling bare feet. Above you, hanging on ropes like bunches of strange fruit, or straddling beams that span the room, is all manner of riding gear; bridles and straps and brasses and brushes and strops and whips and buckets and saddle blankets and there, on the beams, the saddles themselves, all soft hide and gleaming steel and intricate stitching and wonderful swirling folds and tucks and planes and edges. And from them all rains down on your upturned face the sweet rich perfume of oiled new leather. You breathe deeply and become aware of other smells; powdery crushed maize and dusty beans spilling from open sacks, clean woolen blankets reeking of newness, cottony bolts of cloth, candle wax, cooking oil, floor polish, dust, dogs, warmth, sweat, people.

Then your eyes adjust to the gloom and you begin to take in the dimensions of the large room with its massive wooden counter sandwiched between the smooth wooden floor and the low hanging ceiling of riding tack. The top of the counter is cluttered with nondescript piles of merchandise, but what catches your eye is the flash of light that bounces off the chrome and curved glass candy containers. They look so sleek and modern perched there on top of the counter that you almost expect them to hold something more than candy - but how hard it is to envision that something when your experience is so limited. You're drawn towards the chrome and glass and its enticing contents, noticing as you approach that the walls behind the counters consist of floor-to-ceiling shelves stacked solidly with cans, boxes, blankets and other goods, the various piles separated at times by painted metal posters from which stare jovial faces whose gleaming teeth and ruby lips and flashing eyes urge you to smoke Springbok cigarettes and wash whiter with Surf and remove that headache with Aspro and drink Machache No.1 for Health.

In later years you will come to know that Madison Avenue is a million miles removed from the sophistication of this advertising but right now you're giddy with the glamour of it all. And you're ready to make a selection from the candy containers and your palms are damp and your lips are dry. Everything under the glass looks wonderfully glutinous and sugary and greasy and powdery in naked primary colors, promising an orgy of sweet satisfaction. After an agony of indecision you at last make your purchase, you clutch your little brown paper bags with their precious contents, and you head back towards the door, back through the shaft of daylight intruding into the room like a magical wand, sparkling and dancing with the shifting dust and the shadow and movement of people.

Outside the light is startlingly bright and the day is still hot and the mangy yellow dogs are still asleep in the shade on the porch and the horse's tails idly swat flies and the children play and the old black scale creaks and clinks as it weighs bales in the corner.

But your soul feels rich and your senses swim from the experience of the wonderland behind you and you know nothing will ever excite you as much.

My innocence was elemental as a butterfly, overflowing with sensations like this. All of my charmed existence was a tuneful dance; a taste, a smell, a touch, a fright, a joy, a tear. Life was a trading store's delights or the warm sun's embrace and the powdery smell of dusty courtyards or the close cool depths of eroded stream beds and the damp silky touch of sleek clay oxen. Life was the smell of animals, of people, of leather, of fresh-warm milk and of warm baked bread and cut flowers in a glass bottle and red wax polish on a cool brick porch and rich soup bubbling in a big black pot on a wood-burning stove in a wide kitchen that smelled mostly of ash and biscuits.

Life was a force that filled my fresh green shoots and fused my tender rhythms to the rhythms of the universe.

Life was a horse, huge and muscled and powerful, with soft brown eyes and a gentle velvet nose. Horses were the noblest, the strongest, the fleetest, the most frightening of all creatures: a worshipful mix of sculpted bone and hide and muscle and soft leather and hard steel and rich aromas; the feel of silky hair and spiky hair and sweat-soaked skin and satin-soft smoothness; the urgent tension of an early-morning ride and the piston-power pounding thrill of strength unleashed in the fluid rushing motion of a gallop. And more than once, breathtaking fright as a girth loosens and the saddle rolls and the horse shies and the legs pump harder and the ground blurs faster and clutching fingers scrabble for a hold before the crunching terrifying smash into hard ground and the cry of fear and pain and then flushed relief that nothing is broken, but a lot of scraping and bruising that will be worn as a proud trophy for the next two weeks.

The ultimate challenge to my six-year-old sense of romance and adventure was to take a long ride, pitting myself alone against the mountains and the elements, strengthened by the presence of my horse and a sure faith in my own courage and daring. After much debate with my parents it was agreed I could make a two-day journey across a small mountain ridge that separated neighboring trading stations. It was a fine challenge, but it was ultimately made possible only by the fact that I was everywhere surrounded and protected by a warm community of friendly tribes people to whom I was the special white child. All whom I met or passed on the journey knew me or knew of me from their always-reliable voice-messaging system that reported my plans up and down the trails days in advance of my departure and recorded my actual progress mile by mile. Even as my parents sat in the gathering darkness of their home porch on my first night away, they could hear the message coming from afar, carried from mouth to ear to hill to dale, reporting that I had safely reached the shepherd's cave and was even now asleep among the sheep and goats. By the time I reached my destination on the following day there was a radio message waiting from my parents, congratulating me on a safe arrival.

I was hardly aware of the invisible network that protected me on the journey. Instead, my youthful ego fed on the evidence of my knightly prowess and made my courage stronger. It was only many years later that I came to wonder at that unique time when it was possible for a white child to be launched alone into Africa's protective bosom - a brief interlude between the former tension of pioneering expansion and the latter conflict brought on by the impulse for freedom from white exploitation. When the simmering urge for liberty at last reached my corner of the world and I was forced as a conscripted police reservist to patrol the riot-stricken black ghetto that bordered my home town, I often recalled that long ride of my childhood and wondered with more than a touch of irony if the people I confronted on patrol were the sons and daughters of those who had once sustained me and made me strong in my time of innocence and vulnerability.

CHAPTER FIVE
Awareness

The defining moment that gave birth to my metamorphosis from patriotic white South African to radical anti-government activist came early. The year was 1971 and I had just completed three months of grueling basic training as part of the compulsory 12-month military service required of all white males. A central feature of the training was constant indoctrination to impress on our young minds the notion that we were part of the roughest, toughest military machine in the world, an invincible colossus that was Africa's last bastion against invading communist hordes.

Armed with an image of myself as the ultimate warrior I eagerly accepted a posting to an infantry regiment that was bound for the Caprivi Strip. This was South Africa's front line in its battle against Swapo, a guerilla organization intent on liberating South West Africa from white rule. I was excited at the prospect of getting into a real shooting war.

Tension mounted as our convoy of 10 trucks crawled slowly towards the battle zone, its pace determined by the speed of the minesweepers that led the way. This was wild country, far from the trappings of civilization, and the dense bush split by the narrow and dusty road gave ample cover to the terrorists we had been told were lurking nearby. There was little talking as my section crouched in the back of a green-painted Bedford truck, nervously fingering the triggers of our semi-automatic rifles. Then we came to a river and the convoy stopped.

As I dismounted from my truck I could see that the first two vehicles in the convoy were already loaded onto a pontoon that would haul them across the river. All around me troops were clambering to the ground and standing in little groups, waiting for instructions. Then somebody made a break for the river, tossing his uniform and rifle aside before plunging into its cool depths. A mad scramble followed and soon the river was filled with shouting, laughing and cavorting men who only moments before had been a tense and disciplined group of soldiers. I looked around for our officers and saw them standing off to one side, beers in hand, grinning at the scene in the water.

"Something's wrong here," I muttered softly to myself.

If Swapo had been tracking our progress we would be sitting ducks in the event of an attack, with our convoy divided on both sides of the river and its protective screen of troops totally vulnerable in their happy swimming hole. I seemed to be the only soldier still armed and in uniform, so I walked over to where the officers and noncoms stood in their jovial huddle and quietly asked a corporal if we should not be concerned about the presence of Swapo.

"Nah," he said, taking a long pull on his beer while giving me a quizzical stare over the rim of the can. "Don't sweat it man. Those kaffirs are too stupid and too scared to attack us."

I stared blankly at him as he wiped his mouth with the back of his hand. My mind was replaying the briefings we had been given: the enemy's objectives, the enemy's tactics, the number of armed confrontations, and the number of dead and wounded.

Was it all a lie? Was this an imaginary war we were fighting?

Looking around, and then indicating the festive scene with a sweep of my arm, I probed the corporal a little further: "Well, corp, they may be stupid and they may be scared, but all it needs is one guy armed with a slingshot to do some real damage here because nobody's paying any attention to this war."

A look of irritation crossed the man's face as he spat his answer at me: "Now you listen, troop. Don't go playing the bloody general here; we don't need you to tell us how to fight this war. I'm telling you these Swapo kaffirs are scared of us and all they're good for are sneak attacks when they think we're vulnerable. So you just go and join your friends in a little swim and let those who know what they're doing worry about the war!"

The rich irony of the corporal's answer was so vivid that I said nothing, waiting for him to digest the implication of his own words. But he took my silence as evidence that I was convinced by his argument and with a curt wave of his hand he indicated that our discussion was over.

Later that afternoon, with the river crossing safely behind us, a second incident occurred to seal the disillusionment in my deeply troubled mind. Our convoy had pulled into a wide-open area where the captain ordered us to prepare camp for the night, marshalling the trucks into a loose semi-circle. Then as I watched from a short distance away he called a second convoy that had been following about five miles behind us, on his field radio. But all that emitted from the radio's speaker was loud static. After several fruitless minutes of barking call signs and waiting for a reply, the officer turned to a lieutenant beside him and wondered aloud at what the problem might be.

"I've been talking to them all day and I don't understand why I can't raise them now," he said, frustration evident in his voice. "Do you think Swapo could be jamming this transmission? Maybe the convoy is under attack?"

The plausible questions were asked in a casual tone that indicated the captain hardly accepted them as a possibility, and I was again gripped by the same sense of unreality that I had experienced earlier in the day. Having witnessed the chaos of the river crossing I was entirely willing to believe that if there had been a Swapo scout anywhere near us, he and his comrades were now making hay with the second convoy. The prospect was unsettling, and I watched the captain closely as he contemplated his options.

The supreme arrogance and stupidity of the officer's next move left me stunned. Talking loudly into the mouthpiece of his radio, he gave the necessary call signs and then outlined his plan, speaking blindly into the ether.

"Listen, I can't hear you guys, but if you can hear me, here's what we're going to do. It's essential that you join up with me tonight because I don't have enough vehicles or men to set a secure defensive perimeter. Here follow my exact coordinates so that you can find us even after it gets dark. Again, here is my position…"

And with that, the captain gave the precise coordinates of our location.

I felt sick. If the enemy were monitoring the open transmission, we would all be dead by morning.

Later that night I manned a listening post about 200 yards from our camp, my ears straining into the darkness to catch the sound of a stealthily approaching enemy. The second convoy had joined us shortly after dark and our increased numbers no longer made us a soft target, but I could not shake a sense of deep-seated unease that came from an awareness that my life was in the hands of incompetent superior officers. Despite my sleepiness I was determined to do my bit to ensure the safety of my comrades.

It was scary out there, all alone, with the typical night sounds of the African bush pressing on me from every side. There was no moon but the stars hung bright and close as usual, providing just enough illumination to detect the shapes of trees and thick bushes. About an hour into my two-hour watch as I crouched in the snug thicket I had chosen for my hiding place, a new sound intruded on my heightened senses. It was the stealthy noise of delicately breaking twigs and brushing leaves, still a long way off, but coming closer. I cocked my head to one side and closed my eyes, straining all my hearing towards that one sound until it was clear to me that something; several somethings were headed my way. The skin tingled on the back of my neck and my breathing came faster as I peered desperately into the gloom, trying to detect the Swapo terrorists who might be upon me at any moment. Should I run, yelling, back to the camp, warning of the impending attack? Should I fire a warning shot? Should I make myself as small as possible until the terrorists were right on top of me and then ambush them? I tried to remember my instructions from the corporal earlier that evening but my mind was frozen in panic.

Then just as I decided to ease myself out of the thicket and steal back to the camp, I realized in horror that the enemy was right there with me. One second the gloom was empty and in the next second huge menacing shapes began to materialize all around me. With a start I realized it was a herd of elephants, browsing their way gently along in the darkness, and if I did not move immediately I was liable to be crushed underfoot. Back-tracking as quickly as I could without alarming the enormous animals, I hurried to the camp and reported breathlessly to the corporal what I had seen.

He seemed ready to upbraid me for my stupidity when, suddenly, there they were, ambling into the open area where our trucks were drawn into a tight defensive circle; a herd of at least thirty elephants who seemed to acknowledge our presence by turning away from us towards a dark stand of trees at the far end of the field. We watched in silence as they passed, amazingly quiet for their size and numbers, until they disappeared from our sight.

Thankfully, the corporal excused me from further watch duty, sending a relief man out instead, and I crawled tiredly onto my ground sheet under one of the trucks. The thought came to me then that if the elephants had indeed been Swapo, and if they had been armed with mortars, the ring of twenty vehicles and more than 200 sheltering men with not a single foxhole among them would have been sitting ducks. But I was too weary to worry much about it at that point and within seconds I was asleep.

The next morning I cast about restlessly for answers to the previous day's events, trying to understand the cavalier attitudes of professional soldiers whose actions were so entirely unprofessional. When the explanation came to me at last it left me with a hollow feeling in the pit of my stomach that was to remain with me, in varying degrees of intensity, for the next 25 years of my life.

These people were motivated by a blind arrogance born out of their absolute conviction that the enemy they faced - specifically, a black enemy - was something less than human and rational and therefore not worthy of the slightest acknowledgement or respect.

Even as I articulated this thought it became clear to me that it had been forming in my subconscious for months, perhaps years. In particular, the barracks and parade ground talk that accompanied the arduous weeks of basic military training had etched an uncomfortable tattoo on my mind - the constant, almost ritualistic, references to "uppity" kaffirs (the South African equivalent of nigger) and how they would be disciplined, beaten, shot, subdued, subjugated or otherwise humiliated by superior whites. Implied in all of this bombastic posturing was the notion that any black person who dared question white superiority deserved whatever he had coming to him - and it surely wouldn't be pleasant.

"We'll show them who's boss!" was almost a mantra, given special emphasis by the multiplied killing implements of a well-equipped military machine.

I was appalled at the stark implications of this suddenly concrete realization. Like it or not, my white skin and the uniform I wore made me one of them. In that moment I reached a decision that would effect the course of the rest of my life: In every practical way possible I would distance myself from such mindless racism.

If I had known then where this decision would lead me and the price it would exact, I might have been somewhat less emphatic in the promise to myself.

A first test came barely a week later when one of our patrols walked into an ambush and two men were wounded. As we discussed the incident in our barracks that evening I mildly ventured the observation that perhaps the enemy we faced was neither as weak nor as stupid as we supposed. My comments were greeted first with incredulity, and then with anger. The argument finally ended with repetition of the familiar refrain, "Just wait - we'll show them who's boss!"

Convinced that our blindly bombastic leaders would sooner or later get some of us killed, and not willing to lay down my life for a cause that I now considered highly suspect, I avoided the possibility of any further direct contact with the enemy by volunteering to drive a supply truck. The remaining months until my discharge moved painfully slowly while my attitude and military bearing both gradually deteriorated to the point that I was as happy to leave my comrades as they were to see me go.

For the next two years I worked as a wildcat coal driller, a brutally tough job that appealed to me because the money was good and most of my time was spent camping in remote areas. Within days of being introduced to a drilling rig for the first time I was assigned my own four-man crew, a tough and savvy team of black men who seemed cheerful enough about working for a 19-year-old kid who knew absolutely nothing about the job but enjoyed the one qualification that apparently made him superior to them in every respect: a white skin. In return for their backbreaking labor the men earned $20 a month and free food, housing and medical coverage.

It wasn't long before my team was setting impressive new records for the amount of feet drilled each day and my consistently superior performance attracted the attention of managers, foremen and veteran drillers. For each of them I had the same answer as I pointed to my crew: "It's not me, it's them."

"But how do you get them to work so hard?" was the standard response.

"I split my bonus with them for every foot we drill."

"You do what? That's crazy, man. Don't you know that if you pay these kaffirs too much they'll become lazy and stop working?"

"Yeah," I would respond sarcastically. "I've noticed that. But isn't it amazing how my wells get drilled quicker and deeper than anyone else's, and I have record-low equipment breakdowns, and none of my crew ever call in sick?"

Then I would offer the coup de grace: "I'll tell you something else I do - instead of sitting in my caravan issuing orders, I work alongside the men as one of the team. We get a lot more done that way."

With this information the incredulity of my hearers would be total and I was left to marvel at the extraordinary depths of their blind prejudice that allowed them to reject the hard evidence before their eyes. To my knowledge, nobody else ever adopted my methods and I continued to set new records month after month, until I decided it was time to try my hand at something else.

My next job as a trainee hotel manager brought me into contact for the first time with another ugly facet of life in South Africa: the monolithic, brutal and aggressive Department of Bantu (black) Administration. These were the defenders of the dike that held back the black hordes from swamping the sunny white lifestyle enjoyed by a privileged 10 percent of the population. Through ruthless enforcement of the so-called "Pass Laws" - so named because every black person in South Africa had to carry an identity passport that told his life story - the Department regulated and vigorously enforced where blacks would live, how and where they would be educated, where they could work and the kind of work they could do, how much money they could earn, and in some cases, whom they could marry, and when. It was a brutally repressive system that nevertheless stayed below the radar of most white South Africans who seldom gave a second thought to the fact that they always had available an abundant supply of inexpensive and subservient black labor to execute their every indolent whim.

The Department was particularly aggressive in Cape Town, that beautiful city that hangs like an extravagant jewel on the lobe of Africa. There is something wonderful and magical about Cape Town, something almost otherworldly in the dense compactness of its beauty and the surrounding countryside; craggy mountains, rolling valleys, pristine beaches, lucid seas and a sky that often sparkles like champagne. Although manmade, the city itself and nearby towns and villages all share a special quality of belonging to the land, as if the architects who conceived them were mindful of a sacred trust to avoid the desecration of so much natural perfection. The intensity of all this beauty happily conferred a softer spirit on the area, quite different in quality from the harsh and more aggressive tone that commanded South Africa's further expanses. Yet the presence of black Africans was hardly tolerated in Cape Town and its environs.

It was the official contention that Bantu people - those of Negroid descent - had not yet settled the southern tip of the continent when the first Dutch settlers arrived in 1652, and almost since that time succeeding white administrations had followed a policy to admit them to this special place only under special circumstances, as menial laborers paid starvation wages to do the work that nobody else would do at any price.

Gugulethu was designated their home, a mean depressing enclave established a safe but convenient distance from the heart of Cape Town, seldom seen by whites. In 1993 it would achieve brief notoriety in America following the brutal murder there of Amy Biehl, a 26-year-old Fulbright scholar dedicated to hastening South African democracy. But to the thousands of so-called undocumented workers drawn from impoverished black "homelands" in the interior of the country by the irresistible magnet of work in the sprawling metropolitan area surrounding Cape Town, Gugulethu was an unattainable dream. These people existed in crude shelters they built for themselves among the sand dunes that formed the neck of the Cape Peninsula. At first, the community there was scattered enough to be invisible. But as the numbers of squatters grew the government suddenly woke up to the fact that they presented a serious problem, not only because the rapidly expanding squatter camp lacked the most basic services to sustain healthy life, like running water and sewerage disposal, but more importantly because they represented a serious challenge to the government's authority to control who lived where.

When warnings to vacate the squatter camp went unheeded, the official reaction was typically brutal and efficient: bulldozers were dispatched to flatten the area and make it uninhabitable. By this time the camp was dubbed "Crossroads" for a major highway intersection that bordered one side, and it quickly became a symbol of the struggle against apartheid's monolithic rule.

I found myself swept up in the rising tide of angry opposition to the government's heavy-handed actions to clear the area, but my heady idealism received a rude setback on the day I joined a human chain of mostly white protesters who linked arms and vowed to die rather than allow the bulldozers to enter a section of the camp slated for demolition. Scowling police and Bantu Administration officials stood to one side as two enormous bulldozers clanked towards the frail zinc and tarpaper shacks protected by several hundred protesters. The size of the demonstration and the presence of newspaper reporters meant that this day's encounter would be largely symbolic. Or so we thought, until the bulldozers dipped their massive steel blades into the sandy soil immediately ahead of where we stood, and kept on coming. As the earth began to fold over in huge waves that threatened to bury us, if the blades did not cut us in two, I happened to catch a glimpse of the bulldozer operator on the machine to my left. He was smiling. Suddenly the line of protesters broke and ran. As I fled with the others in a mad scrambled for safety I was aware of the derisive jeers and laughter issuing from the ranks of the law enforcement officials who applauded our flight with undisguised glee.

Eventually, a sort of compromise was hammered out over Crossroads: a limited number of shacks could remain and basic services would be provided, if the residents agreed to police their own area and keep other squatters out. At the time it seemed to me like a victory for the government.

During the next several years of my stay in Cape Town, as I cut my teeth on the hotel trade and later became part owner of an upscale restaurant, I found myself in an almost daily running battle with the brown-suited apartheid enforcers from the Department of Bantu Administration who went about their business of pursuing and deporting undocumented workers with an almost religious zeal. For the most part the men I encountered were mean, petty, ignorant of life outside their narrow purview, and brutally efficient in the enforcement of the myriad oppressive regulations that made up the sum of their existence. Their hostility to black people and to anyone who appeared remotely sympathetic towards black people seemed fuelled by their frighteningly intense conviction that they were not dealing with human beings but with an inferior yet dangerous sub-species of life with whom they were locked in a deadly struggle for dominion in South Africa. Because of their innate sense of superiority they did not fear individual blacks; they feared their vast numbers and the constant threat this posed to their security. The solution they employed in dealing with this threat was to treat blacks in the same way a handler would treat valuable but dangerous animals - give them food and water, keep them on a very short leash, control their every movement, and never turn your back on them.

Generally, the system worked very well. Occasionally, however, an irritating ruffle would mar its seamless operation: some whites would help some blacks to circumvent the race laws. These whites were viewed in two categories - those who were merely ignorant and motivated by greed or stupidity, and those who where impelled by a baffling and sinister desire to view blacks as equals, or at least as sentient human beings. The former category of whites were patiently educated to understand the proper role of blacks in society and to aid in the enforcement of the laws necessary to ensure the fulfillment of that role. The latter category was seen as weird aberrations that should be approached like a highly toxic substance: handle with care until safely neutralized.

In all of their dubious doings the Bantu Administration officials were ably supported by the police, whose traditional crime-fighting role played second fiddle to the far more important requirement to maintain white rule, at any cost and by any means necessary. The unholy alliance between these two brutal arms of the white regime ensured that the life of the average black person in South Africa was a miserable struggle for survival against an infrastructure that greeted him with hostility at every turn.

To the whites who employed black people in almost any capacity, as gardener, maid, factory laborer, dish washer, cook, cleaner, ditch digger, office messenger, shop assistant, clerk or in any other approved menial occupation, the "Pass Laws" were an intimidating and expensive hurdle that had to be crossed repeatedly. It was illegal to employ someone who did not possess the requisite pass to work in a specific area and at a specific occupation; when a properly documented worker was employed, that person had to be registered with the authorities, for a fee. When the same person became unemployed, the authorities had to be notified. If an undocumented worker was employed, and the authorities uncovered the crime, heavy fines ensued for both employer and employee.

Stringent employment conditions also had to be met: the nature of the work to be done - because most skilled jobs were reserved for whites - the amount of money to be paid - usually a maximum was stipulated, not a minimum - and where the employee would live. This latter control always had heartbreaking consequences because workers who were housed by their employers were strictly barred from having their families with them. The proper, approved, place for families and dependants of workers was back in the "homelands", wherever that might be, a hundred miles away or a thousand miles away. One of the horrifying consequences of this particularly nasty little prohibition was the rampant spread of aids and venereal diseases, especially throughout the huge mining sector which employed hundreds of thousands of migrant laborers who were separated from their wives and children for up to a year at a time.

I saw the brutal effect of this law for the first time when I worked as an assistant manager at Lanzerac Hotel, a beautiful former wine farm in the pristine town of Stellenbosch, some 40 miles from Cape Town. Most of our employees were mixed-race, or "colored" - their official apartheid designation - and they had no Pass Law problems because the Western Cape area where Stellenbosch and Cape Town were located was considered their homeland. But in addition to our colored chefs and waiters and bellhops, we employed some black maids, all properly documented. The husband of one of the maids also worked in Stellenbosch, as a salesman for a liquor company. This was an unusually prestigious and well-paid job for a black man, made necessary by the large number of illegal black drinking establishments - shebeens - in the Western Cape. His name was Frank and he regularly visited his wife in the room provided to her by the hotel, often spending the night with her. I was aware this was happening and happily approved. But Bantu Administration did not.

Acting on a tip from a jealous co-worker they raided our employee living quarters in the early pre-dawn hours, and found Frank in bed with his wife. Aroused by the banging on doors and shouting that accompanied the raid I rushed to see what was happening and found the half-naked couple being unceremoniously shoved into the back of a waiting police van. Demanding an explanation, I was confronted by a very angry official who informed me that my hotel was "in big trouble" for harboring illegal persons.

"These aren't illegal persons," I protested. "This woman works here. All her papers are in order, and that man is her husband. I demand that you release them immediately."

"That man has no right to be here," the official snarled in reply. He was a large man with a florid face and sported the brown suit of a Bantu Administration agent. I was incensed by his overbearing arrogance.

"That man is the legal husband of this woman and has every right to be here," I shouted. "Who the hell do you think you are to come here in the middle of the night and invade our privacy this way? This hotel is private property and I demand that you release these people immediately and get out of here!"

Ominously, the official was unfazed by my angry reaction. He stared coldly at me for a moment and then slowly and deliberately drew a large pistol from the holster on his hip. Shoving the pistol into my chest, he sneered at me and said, "Listen, sonny, these people are under arrest. Your hotel is going to be fined. And if you don't shut up I'll put you in the back of that van too."

Not waiting for my reply he turned and called to the small group of officials and police who had been watching our exchange with delighted smirks, "Okay, men, let's go."

Within seconds their small convoy of three vehicles roared out of the hotel gates and I was left to contemplate my impotent rage. A week later after all the necessary documents had been filed and the fines had been paid and the assurances had been given that the crime of a wife cohabiting with her husband in an unapproved manner would not be repeated, the couple were released from jail and returned to work. I could not tell how deeply scarred they were by the experience. They did not discuss it with me. I came to understand that this messy incident was the price a black person paid for a good job and the best thing to do was to keep your head down and your mouth shut.

Several years later I found myself in a junior partnership as the on-site manager of Benham Restaurant, located in the upscale, oak-lined Cape Town suburb of Newlands. One of the unexpected hazards of the job was employing unskilled laborers - dish washers, floor cleaners and the like. Blacks were the only people willing to do this poorly paid, unattractive work, and often they did not possess the proper documentation. Even if they did, the headaches involved with the Bantu Administration Department were a burden often shunned - checking papers, registration, paying fees, then notification two weeks later that the employee had found better employment and moved on, thus repeating the tiresome process with the next worker. It was a lot easier to employ someone because you liked the look of him and simply ignore the standard employment challenge, "May I see your pass, please?"

Unfortunately, I seemed to be on some sort of Bantu Administration hit list, possibly because of my earlier encounters at Lanzerac Hotel, or my involvement with the Crossroads protests. Whatever the cause, Benham Restaurant was a regular target of pass raids by the brown-suited upholders of white civilization. Such was the arrogance and insensitivity of these officials that they often conducted their raids on Saturday nights, our busiest time. They would simply march into the restaurant and loudly ask for the manager, then demand to see all the employees and their matching documentation. On several occasions, when we could not hide our undocumented workers quickly enough, they would be dragged out of the restaurant past the politely averted gaze of the white diners. Once, the mayor of Cape Town was enjoying a meal when a raid took place and I appealed to him for help. He helplessly shrugged his shoulders: some things in South Africa just could not be changed. We were all prisoners together of the system.

CHAPTER SIX
Harry

Harry provided an entertaining yet ultimately tragic highlight of my time in Cape Town. He was a businessman, an entrepreneur with an unerring eye for spotting moneymaking opportunities. Orphaned and abandoned on Gugulethu's mean streets at the age of ten, his ready wit and boundless often-groundless optimism helped him to survive and prosper against enormous odds. His smile and quick retort were trademark responses to every challenge. He was utterly fearless, even of the police, who never were denied the full benefit of his boyish charm.

Harry was the sort of person who always looked well dressed, whether he was wearing overalls or a three-piece suit. Clothes hung well on his compact frame and somehow his sparkling inner spirit seemed to rub off on them and make the folds appear a little neater, the creases that much sharper.

I met him when he rescued me from the big oak tree in my front yard. An unfriendly lightening bolt sheared off half its massive bulk and left the splintered remains leaning drunkenly against my house. Before the professional tree felling service arrived at my request to estimate the cost of removing the tree, Harry came.

"Boss has got a problem with his tree," he stated flatly, after knocking at the front door and foregoing the usual formal introductions when I answered.

"Yes, I have."

"I fix it for you."

I looked him over. A young man with an open, serious face, level eyes creased by laugh lines at the corners and a generous mouth flashing sets of even teeth. He wore spotless neat blue denim pants and a matching work shirt.

"How much?"

He mentioned a price roughly half of what I expected to pay. Intrigued, I asked him, "How do I know you can do the job?"

Prepared for this question, the itinerant tree feller produced a neatly folded sheet of paper containing a list of names and addresses that read like a summary of the Cape Town social register.

"I fix trees for them all," he said. "You can phone."

"How did you know my tree needed fixing?"

"The garden boy next door told his brother. His brother works for me."

"Okay," I said, "you've got the job. What's your name?"

"Harold Benjamin Mashabela."

He spoke each word slowly and formally as if, by deliberate emphasis, to give substance to the person behind the name. Then he flashed a broad smile and added: "But everybody calls me Harry."

A few days later Harry returned with a small truck and half a dozen assistants dressed in identical blue uniforms. They were armed with an impressive array of motorized power saws and made short work of reducing the tree to neat piles of firewood.

As I handed over the cash I asked Harry where he had learned his trade.

"A white boss teach me."

"And now you're your own boss?"

A flicker of pride crossed his face as he answered, "Yes."

My frequent confrontations with Bantu Administration officials and police over the employment of blacks in my restaurant had made me familiar with the pervasive regulations that touched every facet of their lives and seemed designed to discourage them from participating in any meaningful way in the bounty enjoyed by the white community. I was almost certain that a black businessman like Harry would be operating without official approval, and I wondered how he got away with it.

"Is your business legal?" I asked.

Until now our conversation had been stilted, somewhat formal, in the usual manner of black and white encountering each other for the first time and warily testing the boundaries between them. But at this question Harry threw back his head and gave me a look of quizzical insolence tempered somewhat by his flashing grin.

"Why do you want to know? Are you from police?" he shot back.

"No! No," I replied, suddenly confused and sheepish at being slapped down for prying too closely into his affairs. "No, I'm sorry, I didn't mean to be rude. It's just that black entrepreneurs aren't a common sight around here and I'm intrigued at how you set up your business."

"No matter," he said cheerfully, relaxed now that he had established we were equals. Then he added with a sly grin, "All my papers are in order. All the little pieces of paper that make the Boere happy have got all the right stamps and the right names and the right numbers so I can just be a happy little kafferkie helping the white boss to make his garden grow."

"The Boere?" I was unfamiliar with the term.

"Yah. The Boere. The police. The ones who aren't happy if they find you in a white place and your papers aren't right. But my papers are always right!"

I had the distinct impression that Harry was hinting at the possession of forged documents, but I was reluctant to pursue that thought after his earlier reaction to my questioning. Instead, we talked at some length about the nature of his work and the people it brought him into contact with. He was full of amusing and incisive observations on the lifestyle of Cape Town's white society and I found his cheerful confidence and vibrant inner strength a refreshing contrast to the usual obsequious or sullen black facade.

On impulse I invited him to dinner. I wanted to get to know him better and to better understand the currents that made up his life in Gugulethu, a few miles and a world away.

A week later he came to dinner at my home. It would have been impossible to entertain him at my restaurant because blacks were legally barred from entry there, except as workers. Such was the confusing and artificial nature of black/white relations in South Africa that I wasn't even sure that it was legal to let him into my home as a guest, but I had no intention of asking the police for information on that score.

Pamela, his sometime companion, accompanied Harry. She was an effervescent brassy woman whose bold humor and heavy township slang complemented Harry's fast-paced chatter. They were both immaculately dressed and informed me immediately that they planned to take me to a nightclub in Gugulethu after we had eaten. There I could experience first-hand why Cape Town's shabby dormitory town was known to its party crowd as Paradise.

Apart from his clothes, Harry had undergone a more startling transformation. In our opening conversation his language had been typically broken and heavily accented, but now he spoke with a fluid township jive that reflected his true street-wise education and ambitions.

He laughed when I pointed this out.

"Hey, man, do you think that you or any of your tight-assed white friends would hire a black man who came to their front door sounding like he might be smarter than they are? Forget it. Remember, the first thing a successful businessman learns is to give a customer what he wants, and what you whites want are nice respectful darkies working for you."

As we sat down to dinner I asked him if he did not resent playing this double role.

"Hey, I'm happy, man," he replied. "I've got the system all worked out. The only occasional hassle comes from the Boere, but if you know how to keep your cool and how to handle them, it's no problem.

"It's you whiteys who have the problems. Always looking over your shoulders or hiding behind your high walls in your boring suburbs, wondering when the revolution is going to come. You're all so scared about tomorrow that you can't enjoy life today.

"Now, take me. I live in Paradise. The Gugulethu Free Zone. The only whites brave enough to poke their noses in there are the police, and they don't do it very often, so we do our own thing. The music there is better, the booze is better and the chicks are better than anywhere else on earth. I tell you, man, if you've got money in your pocket and a China-eyes wrapped around you, you've got it all!"

I learned that a China-eyes was a Mercedes Benz, the ultimate status symbol. And I was only mildly surprised to hear that Harry owned one in partnership with a friend.

"Yeah, it's parked right outside," he said, grinning hugely, "because we're going to take you to Paradise in style!"

Harry explained that during the week his partner operated the car as a high-class taxi, mainly for funerals and similar formal events. On weekends, they took turns using it for pleasure.

"Of course," he added with a smile, "we seldom take it out of Gugulethu. That's asking for trouble. When you're out of the Free Zone and into enemy territory you've got to be careful, man. It's dangerous out there.

"If you want to travel someplace else without being hassled by the Boere you better go in a little kaffir car that doesn't attract too much attention. And don't dress too loud. The Boere don't like white kaffirs and they can make things hot for you, so you gotta take it easy."

Harry laughed.

"But if you want some real hairy entertainment then you get out the China-eyes, put on your best clothes and your shades, pack your pass, your driver's license, your car ownership papers and anything else that proves you're a free, legal, law-abiding citizen of this great land of ours, and you head out into the country. The Boere will stop you for sure. They can't believe that such a cool-looking little kaffirkie isn't a thief, or worse, a member of the ANC. And then things get really interesting for a while."

Harry stared reflectively into his wineglass. We had been drinking steadily for several hours and four empty wine bottles attested to the success of the meal. He slurred his words slightly as he made the next statement with a note of both sorrow and defiance in his voice:

"You know, I've been treated like a mangy cur dog by the police and the Bantu Admin people and by ordinary white people so many times that I've often wondered why God hated me so much to let me be born in this country with a black skin. Then there are other times when I wouldn't want to be anybody else but who I am. I'm Harry Benjamin Mashabela. My mother was a washerwoman and I don't know who my daddy was. It doesn't matter. I'm here now. I'm me. And I'm going to stay on topside no matter what the Boere do to me, because I'm better than they are."

With that, Harry beamed at me once more and said, "Come on, I'm going to show you what you've been missing all your miserable white life!"

But I had to decline the invitation. Several bottles of wine and a rich pepper cream sauce on a very rare steak were now locked in violent combat somewhere deep inside me and I asked Harry if we could reschedule the visit for another time. The look of disappointment that clouded his face was quickly buried under his flashing smile. We parted warmly. I never saw him again.

Pamela called a week later. The police had stopped them on the ride home, at the entrance to Gugulethu, where roadblocks were often established to check for contraband being smuggled into or out of the township. The roadblocks also discouraged casual visits from whites, who required a special permit to enter the black area. On this occasion the well-honed police instincts for smelling a rat down every new drainpipe were aroused by the discovery of a highly articulate black man behind the wheel of the executive car. Harry's own instincts were dulled by the effects of the wine and he made the fatal mistake of stubbornly arguing his right to refuse a search. When he was curtly ordered to produce his papers and reached for the sleek black leather wallet from the inside pocket of his jacket, it slipped through alcohol-numbed fingers to the floor between his feet. Bending to retrieve it, he made some choice remarks about the ancestry of the policemen confronting him.

They shot him as he sat behind the wheel of his beloved Mercedes Benz.

CHAPTER SEVEN
Ficksburg

My father was a racist, no different from the 6,000 other whites who made up the small conservative community of Ficksburg, my hometown. But he was also a canny businessman who knew a moneymaking opportunity when he saw one, and he saw one in the need to treat the black customers of his wholesale business with dignity and respect.

Shortly after he lured me back home to take over the business and ease him into retirement, he outlined his plan to become a dominant wholesale distributor in a market that extended primarily throughout the neighboring Kingdom of Lesotho.

"There are seven wholesalers in Ficksburg, including us," he said, "and for the most part we all treat our black customers like second-class citizens. But, like it or not, these people are moving quickly towards more political and economic power. Particularly in Lesotho, they're going to be taking over more and more white-owned trading stations and when they do we have to be ready to earn their business."

His vision was very simple, but it represented a radical departure from accepted practice: treat black customers as equals, extend the same credit terms to them that white customers enjoyed, and partner with them in other ways to help their businesses to grow, especially in the early stages when they would be struggling to come to terms with their new identity as entrepreneurs.

"They'll appreciate all the help they get, and when they grow, we will grow," my father declared. "And as more customers switch from the other wholesalers to ourselves - and they will, because those other guys are totally locked into their old racial attitudes - we'll grow even faster."

I needed no encouragement. Not only did it make good economic sense to treat all of our customers alike, it was morally the right thing to do. Besides, Harry's death had left me feeling impotent and angry and I had been glad to leave Cape Town, the bitter memory of the place only partly mollified by the fact that I had met and married Linda there. Now I eagerly embraced the opportunity to make a statement in an area which I fully controlled, my own business.

But the implementation of policies and practices radically at odds with convention was to set a chain of events in motion that eventually brought me into conflict with the entire white community and ultimately placed my life on the line.

It started simply enough, with an invitation to tea. I announced to my employees that henceforth all of our customers would be offered the courtesy of a cup of tea when they visited us, and all would be served out of the same cups. My white employees were appalled.

It was not so much the courtesy of the tea they objected to, but the idea of drinking from a cup that a black person might previously have used. The issue came to a head when I discovered that a white female employee had marked a cup with a dab of red nail polish on its base and then issued instructions that this cup was to be for her exclusive use. One evening after work I spent a few minutes marking all of the teacups in a similar way. It took about a week for the woman to discover my subterfuge and then she confronted me in an apoplectic rage.

Calmly, I asked her how she felt.

"What do you mean, how do I feel?" she spluttered. "I feel terrible. I feel betrayed."

"No," I replied, "I mean, how do you feel physically? Are you well? Have you been to see a doctor this week?"

The woman gave me a befuddled stare.

"What in heaven's name are you talking about? My health is fine!"

"Well, then, you clearly have not contracted a life-threatening illness as a result of drinking from a cup that might have been used by a black person. I'm very happy for you. You should be happy too."

But she was not at all happy. Grinding her teeth in anger, she proceeded to describe my pedigree in some considerable detail before declaring that she would no longer work for me, under any circumstances. I was glad to see her go. For good measure, I announced after her departure that our toilet facilities would no longer be segregated. This shocking development was too much even for those white employees who had, albeit reluctantly, submitted to the sharing of teacups, and several more resigned.

I was not overly concerned by this loss of key workers. I believed I would find suitable replacements from the large but unskilled pool of black labor that traditionally languished in menial jobs under the careless domination of whites who often had scant qualifications to lead them, apart from the treasured possession of a white skin.

I was convinced that suitable black candidates needed only a little training and encouragement to perform well as managers and supervisors, and I put my theory to the test by dismissing the incompetent white manager of my retail clothing outlet and appointing a young black woman in his place. Her name was Martha. I watched her closely at work in my warehouse for several weeks before offering her the job. She was bright and hard working, with a wonderfully positive outlook on life.

"Do you think you'll be able to do it?" I asked her.

"I don't know, Boss," she replied, in the halting, deferential way that black people adopted when conversing with their white masters. "But if Boss wants to do this thing I surely would like to try."

"If you will let me train you, you will have no problems," I assured her.

My confidence was based on the fact that during my stint as part-owner of Benham Restaurant in Cape Town, I had acquired valuable experience in training workers who had none of the skills nor cultural experiences necessary to perform well in the myriad busy activities that characterize an upscale dining establishment. Part of the success of the restaurant came from the success I had in turning raw recruits into polished chefs, waiters, wine stewards, cleaners and quality controllers.

I made my mistakes, of course. One of the key lessons learned was not to presume anything and not to view the training from my perspective, but from the perspective of the one being trained. This was especially true when much of the knowledge and skill I imparted was incomprehensible in terms of its cultural content or rational expectation. In other words, I had to find a way to convincingly impart information that made me appear an idiot to my hearers. Sometimes I resorted to demanding precise adherence to my instructions simply because I was the boss!

On one notable occasion I trained a young woman to be a quality controller. Her name was Margaret and she was very keen to accept this position that elevated her far above the level of dishwasher, her first job. As a quality controller in the kitchen it would be her responsibility to check each plate of food before it was passed on to a waiter for final delivery to a diner. Patiently, I showed her how to do it: check the plate for warmth; check for gravy on the edges or bits of food in odd places; check that all the necessary items are present; and lastly, add a light garnish of parsley for effect. Again and again we repeated the procedure until I was satisfied that Margaret did it well. Again and again I repeated the mantra, "You do it this way. No other way. This way."

The time finally came for Margaret to be left alone and I went about my business of circulating amongst the diners to ensure they were all content.

In the restaurant trade one develops a sort of uncanny sixth sense, possibly from interacting closely with people about something as intimate as the food they are eating. Thus, I responded quickly to a little alarm in my head that warned me all was not as it should be. Surveying the crowded dining room I at last spotted a table of four people who looked as if they were about to leave, and I hurried over to them.

"Is everything satisfactory?" I asked, smiling. "Have you enjoyed your meal?"

They replied in unison that the meal had been outstanding. But I caught a little glance between them and probed a little deeper: "Are you sure? Is there anything more I can do for you?"

"Well," said one of the diners, "we were wondering about just one thing that struck us as a little strange."

Alarmed, I waited for the axe to fall. It must have showed on my face because the diner immediately reassured me, "No, really, the whole evening has been very pleasant. But we were wondering why you put parsley on your ice cream and hot chocolate sauce?"

I was mortified and made my apologies before rushing into the kitchen and confronting Margaret, just as she was about to add an artistic sprinkle of parsley to a hot apple pie.

She was mystified by my distress.

"You told me to do this," she said.

"No I didn't! I never told you to put parsley onto ice cream or apple pie or any other dessert, for that matter."

Now Margaret looked thoroughly confused, even a little frightened. Here was the dreaded confrontation with the white boss who issued incomprehensible instructions and then changed them on a whim, and it was always the black subordinate who suffered. That was the way of the world. Resignedly, Margaret hung her head.

"I'm sorry, master, I thought you told me to put this green stuff on all the food. That is what I did. I put it on all the food. You did not tell me to put it on this food but not on that food."

In that moment I saw how ridiculous my position was and my heart went out to this young woman who was trapped by a circumstance she had no way of controlling. For someone to whom the average meal was no more than a single item of food, the very concept of different courses was a mystery. It was all food and it should all be treated the same. Gently, I apologized to Margaret for the misunderstanding and reviewed the whole process with her again. She went on to become one of my key employees.

So by the time I arrived in Ficksburg I had a pretty clear idea of the pitfalls and possibilities in training the people who worked for me, and I had thoroughly demolished to my own satisfaction the prevailing white wisdom that blacks were too stupid to learn any meaningful skills. I had also learned that blacks were not lazy, just demotivated by slave wages and dreadful working conditions. These handicaps were easy to fix.

When I selected Martha to run my retail store and told her how much she would be paid for the job, her jaw dropped. It was three times more than she had previously earned and I knew she would work her heart out for that kind of money. In addition, I outlined a bonus incentive scheme tied to the performance of the store, explaining how the money would be apportioned between her and her staff, and suggested that she call the store employees together to tell them that she was implementing the incentive program. This would give her enormous credibility in their eyes and go some way towards suppressing their skepticism about having a woman for a boss, and a black woman at that!

The expected backlash from the white community was not long in coming. Increasingly angry delegations of customers confronted me in my office, declaring in one way or another that they could no longer support my business because what I was doing was at best foolish and at worst, downright subversive. I even had a courtesy call from the local police chief, who pointedly declined the cup of tea I offered him while urging me to consider the impact of my actions on the peace and good neighborliness of our happy little town. The implication was clear: If blacks were encouraged to see themselves as the equal of whites - which they obviously were not - it might cause them to become dissatisfied with their lot. I ignored all the warnings and watched in delight as Martha blossomed into a dynamic businesswoman. Revenues at the store broke all previous records while losses from theft or the mishandling of goods quickly dropped to zero. The results were so dramatic that a year later I opened a second retail outlet and put a black woman in charge there too. She was no less successful.

Meanwhile, my wholesale business was flourishing as word rapidly spread in the black business community - particularly among the growing number of black trading station owners across the border in Lesotho - about the strange young white man who appeared to be completely color blind. Every white customer I lost was replaced by two black customers, and soon I had to expand my facilities.

Several years after taking full control of the business from my father and finding a partner who would regularly visit our rapidly expanding wholesale customer base while I managed our day-to-day operations, I became active in the local (whites only) chamber of commerce. It offered access to a forum that gave me some weight in my ongoing skirmishes with petty bureaucrats whose myopic enforcement of the myriad's of race-based regulations had a stifling effect on business in general and on my business in particular.

Soon I was invited to join the executive committee of the chamber and the following year became president, primarily because the other members were impressed by the burgeoning success of my various business ventures and the credibility I had established within the black community. Even the most racist of white business owners and managers recognized blacks were indispensable sources of both labor and purchasing power.

So it was almost by accident that I found myself thrust into the role of mediator between two communities totally dependent on each other yet separated by a vast gulf of ignorance, prejudice and mistrust; a gulf created by rigid, all-pervasive laws designed exclusively to ensure the continued domination of whites in a country where they were out-numbered ten-to-one by their black fellow-citizens. It was 1985 and South Africa was about to reap the bitter harvest of 40 years of this repressive white rule. We did not know it then, but we had entered the first stages of a civil war that would see the escalation of wrenching unrest to a level of violence so widespread and so brutal as to make the country almost ungovernable and lead to a black takeover of power within ten years. Tens of thousands of people would lose their lives in the struggle and no town or neighborhood - almost no individual - would emerge unscathed from the conflict. Unwittingly, I was stepping into the red-hot maw of a crucible that would sweep me up in events that were way beyond my ability to control, or even to anticipate.

My introduction to the realities and limitations of white power in the rapidly shifting political landscape came almost immediately after my election as President of the Ficksburg Chamber of Commerce. Within days I found myself locked in discussions with the Administrative Committee of the black township of Meqeleng, the dormitory community situated on a barren hilltop a mile from the outskirts of Ficksburg.

Typical of thousands of other "feeder" communities that were married to every white village, town and city in the country, Meqeleng's population was five times the size of Ficksburg's but enjoyed almost none of the basic infrastructural facilities like utilities, paved roads, parks and shopping centers. It was a depressingly Spartan ghetto that featured row upon identical row of matchbox cinderblock homes interspersed by rutted, garbage-strewn streets. There was hardly a tree in sight. Indeed, almost the only structures that rose above rooftop level were the 50 foot tall security towers that reared like skeletal fingers out of the dust and carried on their gaunt tops the massive incandescent lights designed to beat back the darkness and ensure that subversive or disruptive elements within the generally cowed black population had no place to hide after nightfall.

To look at, Ficksburg was like any small American town. Meqeleng was like the script from a nightmare. But like any nightmare it produced some unexpected twists that would one day create major headaches for the apartheid planners who had dreamed it up.

The brutally practical concept behind townships like Meqeleng was that they provided the minimum conditions necessary to sustain the wellbeing of those whose labor was required by the adjacent white town. As such, they were designed as antiseptic, easily controlled enclaves where blacks would be kept to themselves when they were not actually doing the white man's bidding. Water was not piped into individual homes but to a central facility that might serve as many as a dozen homes. Likewise, electricity was fed into central distribution boxes from which extensions radiated in anonymous clusters. It was a neat ghetto that could be easily locked up and controlled.

The nightmare came when blacks began to organize themselves and turned these same ghettos into fortresses. Their unexpected but very real strength was expressed in many ways. Residents tapped at will into the electricity supply then refused to pay the bills that were delivered to each block of homes. Because the design of the system made it impossible to identify whom, specifically, was using electricity, the only recourse for the white authorities was to turn off the supply. But if they did that the area would be plunged into welcome darkness at night, making the security towers impotent and the watchful eyes of the police blind to all manner of illegal and threatening political activities.

Similarly, residents refused to pay their water bills. But the authorities could not turn off the water and sanitation services because the densely populated ghetto would immediately become a breeder of diseases that would threaten the nearby white community.

Then the stakes were raised when blacks began to systematically destroy administrative facilities like offices and especially schools. But these had to be replaced at enormous expense and then protected by massive police details because the authorities recognized it was essential not only to maintain an official presence in the ghettos but also to keep children off the streets and in schools where they could be better controlled. The impossible scale of the problem began to dawn on the government when the unrest and disruption was duplicated in thousands of ghettos across the land. For blacks, it was blackmail and payback of the sweetest kind.

And it was against this background that I was charged with the task of negotiating with Meqeleng's Administrative Committee to keep the lid on the simmering unrest in that community. But it quickly became apparent to me that the men I was dealing with were merely the appointed puppets of the white regime who enjoyed no credibility and therefore had no power to direct or influence the actions of their own people. Our meetings were exercises in futility; formal, polite occasions where we seldom achieved more than the production of agendas, minutes and resolutions in answer to the increasing evidence of black discontent that took the form of wildcat strikes, boycotts and sabotage.

This situation was intolerable to me and as I cast about in frustration for a workable alternative I stumbled across the real power base in the township, the shadowy and illegal African National Congress.

My introduction to the ANC came in the form of an unannounced visit from a young man whose appearance and demeanor set him apart from any other black person I had ever met. I did not know at the time that I was talking to the president of the local chapter of the banned black political organization whose name to most whites was synonymous with terrorism, communism and revolution. As he sat across from me in my office and casually mentioned that he had heard about the innovative things I was doing in my business and wanted to get to know me, I wondered at his self-confidence.

"Perhaps we can work together," he said, speaking in heavily accented English.

"In what way?" I asked, somewhat unsettled by his direct manner. He gave me a long, cool stare before replying matter-of-factly, "Well, I can tell you that you're not going to get anywhere in your discussions with those puppets on the Administrative Committee about the school boycott. I'm the man to talk to."

"And just who are you?" I shot back, a little irritated by his arrogance.

"Thabo."

Nothing else. Just that. A single word. His name, but much more than his name, his entire identity. Thabo. Take it or leave it.

I was intrigued by his boldness and the total sense of command that he somehow managed to convey in that single small word. On the spur of the moment I decided to go along with him.

"Okay, Thabo, what's the next step?"

"Nothing," he said. "You don't have to do anything. Just go back to your Chamber of Commerce and tell them you've resolved the boycott. It will be over by tomorrow."

"Why are you telling me this?"

"Because you need to establish your credibility as someone who can get things done in the black community. In return, I need a credible contact in the white community whom I can work with, who can get things done for me. Based on what I've seen and heard of you in the last few years, I think you're the man."

I was speechless. This anonymous young black man sitting on my turf was congratulating me on successfully landing a job I had never applied for, and doing it in such a way that I had the distinct impression it was an offer I could not refuse. I probed Thabo for more details and we talked for hours, discovering along the way that we liked each other because neither of us had a high tolerance for empty posturing. It marked the start of a long and intricate relationship in which our destinies became fused into a single purpose, even as our lives sometimes seemed to hang on a slim thread of good luck.

During the next few years, as the weave of South Africa's rigidly ordered society began increasingly to unravel and violence and bloodshed became endemic, I would often meet with Thabo and his secret planning committee several times a week. Between us, we established an underground administration that ensured relatively peaceful and efficient progress in our corner of the world while inexorably advancing the ANC's political agenda. When the ANC was unbanned and became a legitimate political entity in 1990, evidence of the extent of my involvement with the hated "terrorist" organization sent shock waves through the white community. The intimidation campaign against me began shortly thereafter.

A highly incongruous aspect of my life leading up to this time was my service as a conscripted member of the local security forces who dragooned all the available white manpower to bolster their numbers as they conducted increasingly frequent and violent raids, searches and arrests in the simmering black community. The bizarre situation in which I found myself as a recalcitrant "peace" enforcer was typical of South Africa's maddening complexity: I was a known black sympathizer long before my formal involvement with the ANC became evident, yet in the eyes of the local white regime my white skin automatically made me a protector of the status quo. I was never asked if I wanted to serve on a part-time basis in the security forces; I was simply told it was a patriotic duty that carried the penalty of indefinite jail time if refused.

So I found myself serving alongside men who today were my comrades in arms and tomorrow might be my executioners. I despised their arrogant, macho racism and expressed my rebellion against their attitudes and their cause at every opportunity. My resistance was necessarily muted because I could have been thrown in jail, or worse, accused of treason, if my objections were too firmly expressed. I chose instead to be incredibly stupid and slovenly in all that I did. I never reported for duty on time or in the standard-issue military uniform because I persistently ordered uniforms that were hopelessly too big or too small for me. I politely refused to take orders in Afrikaans, which I spoke fluently and which was the universal language of the security forces, exercising instead my right to be addressed in the country's second official language, English. On the one occasion when I was asked to guard prisoners I allowed them to escape, claiming apologetically that they had tricked me.

When assigned at last to duty as a delivery driver, on the assumption that I could do the least amount of damage in that role, I deliberately became hopelessly lost even on the simplest errands. Once I wrecked a vehicle in a spectacular accident.

I was particularly incensed by the violent, abusive way in which the men I served with talked at all times about blacks. It was a special kind of depravity made all the more odious by the fact that it was so casual, almost unconscious. And it was translated into extremely violent action when blacks were encountered in threatening situations: through the psychology of the use of words the unfortunate people these security forces clashed with on a regular basis were not seen as human but as insects, perhaps, or worms; oddities with human faces or human anatomies who excited no compassion, only the occasional vague flash of recognition.

I saw this demonstrated on those few awful nights when I was dragged along with them on raids. The purpose of these raids was never clear, unless it was simply to harass and intimidate. I would do all I could with the limited means at my disposal to frustrate the purpose of my colleagues by inadvertently flashing lights or feigning illness or loudly coughing and blowing my nose. They viewed me as a Jonah and I was assigned the simple task of guarding the vehicles before being barred from raids altogether. But I will never forget the sight of those heavily armed, booted thugs smashing their way through the doors of flimsy homes and rousting out the terrified occupants before ransacking their miserable possessions. On one particularly memorable occasion a naked man and woman were driven out of their home to stand in dazed humiliation in the glare of flashlights as their tormentors laughed and commented on their cowed state.

"Hey, look at her tits," said one, as if he were viewing a lab specimen. Ribald comments followed from the other men. I was standing too far away to see the expression on the woman's face, but her whole body visibly withered under the terrible weight of those unthinking, unfeeling words as she tried hopelessly to cover herself.

A powerful urge swept over me to flip off the safety on my semi-automatic rifle and shoot every one of those men as they stood there. With some difficulty I contained my emotions but I wondered later if I would be able to stop myself the next time. Thankfully, someone in the chain of command eventually thought to relieve me of my duties on the basis that my sorry performance was at best a hindrance to the efficient operation of the security forces. But it was clear to me even then that the official mind found it almost impossible to accommodate the thought that when the chips were down my loyalties would be suspect. I was white and the enemy was black and that should have been the end of the matter.

This strangely myopic mindset was part of the culture of the Afrikaans-speaking ruling elite who were regimented and brainwashed by approved responses to the icons and shibboleths that populated the endlessly repeated folk tales they heard from an early age - at their mother's knee, in school, at political meetings, and thundered from the pulpit every Sunday. Their presence in Africa was not accidental, but part of a divine plan in which they had been specially chosen to bring light to a dark continent, and ultimately, to a dark world. This covenant with God was sealed in a spectacular way when in answer to their fervent prayers a handful of early pioneers had defeated a Zulu army of more than 5,000 warriors. A massive shrine was erected to commemorate the event, relived each year on the solemn Day of the Covenant, where succeeding generations were reminded not to look to their small numbers but to the mighty hand of providence that ever guided them.

My neighbor in Ficksburg provided a startling example of how this thinking worked. Ben Steyn was a local political heavyweight who ran a successful law practice and served as chairman of the Ficksburg branch of the ruling Nationalist Party. We had known each other for many years and often talked over the garden fence. Invariably, when I raised a controversial subject like the disappearance of a political detainee or the injustice of denying black people the right to vote, Ben would simply state that he was not prepared to discuss the matter. It was not an approved topic and the party line was not clear so there was no point in talking about it. Period.

The only time I was able to draw him into a substantial debate was the day I casually told him that I could predict the time and the manner of the collapse of apartheid. This was long before my involvement with the ANC became public knowledge, in the days when apartheid still presented a smooth monolithic facade to the world. The challenge proved irresistible to Ben. He took the bait.

"I suppose you've been looking into a crystal ball?" he retorted.

"It's a little more scientific than that: I've been looking into demographics and economics and I hate to tell you this, Ben, but everything is against you."

"How so?"

I laid out for him the cold facts. The apartheid model was simply unsustainable in the long term because the math did not add up: the dwindling ratio of whites to blacks ran in inverse proportion to the burgeoning needs for cash and loyal white administrators necessary to make the system work.

The moral justification for apartheid was that different groups of people had an intrinsic desire to keep to themselves and this should be both acknowledged and helped by creating structures and facilities that were separate but equal for the different groups. To give effect to this policy the eight or nine major ethnic black groups were each granted their own "homelands" within and alongside the white "homeland". Aside from messy details about minority groups like Asians and East Indians who did not really fit in anywhere, and the fact that the white 10 percent of the population possessed a homeland that covered about 80 percent of the available territory, and the built-in anomaly of the white "tribe" comprising English-speakers and Afrikaans-speakers who were almost two distinct groups, there was a fantastic expense tied to this grand experiment in balkanization.

"That's your Achilles heel," I told Ben. "Sooner or later the money necessary to finance this whole thing is going to run out. The government is counting on a high gold price and foreign investment in the homelands - including the white homeland - to provide a lot of the cash needs, but I suspect that the rest of the world knows this and if the United Nations and the World Bank pulls the plug on investments you're going to be in a heap of trouble."

"Then we'll just have to make sacrifices and provide the money ourselves," Ben protested.

I shook my head in disbelief. "You're asking two million white taxpayers to fund a system for forty million blacks. It can't work," I said. "What's more, those same two million are going to have to provide all the management manpower necessary to administer this monster, robbing people from the productive private sector and further eroding your already small tax base.

"Let's face it Ben, there's just not enough money and there aren't enough whites to make this thing work. So let me tell you when it's all going to end."

"I can't wait," Ben said sarcastically, but I could see the concern in his eyes.

"One day the government is going to wake up and find that it's bankrupt. That will be the day it announces the end of apartheid and tries to cut a deal with blacks to share in the running of the country. But in that moment you're going to reap the whirlwind, you're going to discover that all of these mutually exclusive groups you've so carefully created in pursuit of apartheid are going to turn on each other like starving dogs on a bone and when the dust settles there's going to be nothing left but smoking ruins."

Ben looked at me aghast. "That's a terribly pessimistic view," he grated.

"No. Not pessimistic. Realistic," I answered. "All of the elements are already pretty much in place for this to happen. It's just a matter of time. Not if, but when."

"Well," said Ben, choosing his words carefully, "let's assume for a moment that you're right. Do you see any relief in this grim scenario of yours?"

I though for a moment before replying, "There's one possibility, but it's a remote one. Before that judgement day comes you better pray that somehow, somewhere, a black leader emerges who has the vision and strength of character and sheer force of personality to pull this whole thing together and hold it together until the transition from white minority rule to black majority rule is peacefully completed."

"Do you have anyone in mind?"

I thought again. The government had done such a thorough job of brutally destroying all credible black opposition, including strong black leaders, that the list of candidates was hopelessly small. Certainly, none of the pliant black leaders that the government had nurtured to help implement its policies would fit the bill. There was only one possible candidate.

"Nelson Mandela," I said. "But, frankly, I doubt that even he can pull it off. The man's been in prison so long he's either hopelessly embittered or completely out of touch. I doubt very much that the public mystique surrounding him matches his private image. He's probably little more than a symbol."

As it turned out, that was the only element of my crystal ball gazing that proved incorrect.

CHAPTER EIGHT
Thabo

Thabo Mokele was every white South African's nightmare. Street-smart, self-confident, aggressive, disdainful of white authority and utterly fearless, he was the embodiment of every characteristic that decades of ruthless apartheid policies had been designed to excise from the hearts and minds of those who, by the color of their skin, were officially designated "hewers of wood and drawers of water." His appearance alone was calculated to strike alarm and consternation in whites accustomed to pliant subserviance from anyone with a black skin. Thabo was not a big man but he radiated a big presence, from his wild Afro hairstyle to his coarse pockmarked features and flashing, contemptuous gaze. He was always neatly dressed. And when he walked, he strutted.

It was his walk that told you what he was: proud, free, and dangerous.

When I first met him in 1985 he was barely 28-years-old, an extraordinarily young age for one who played his hazardous role with such aplomb. I was five years older but in many respects I felt that I was his junior; the sheer force of his personality and the price he had paid to keep his spirit free against all the odds, aged him far beyond his years. He knew his life was on the line every day yet he sometimes took tremendous risks to advance the ANC goal of an inevitable transition of power from the white minority to the black majority. Scores of black political activists were murdered each year by a ruthless white regime that was grimly determined to hold on to power and Thabo had no illusions about his fate should he be arrested.

A cornerstone of South African politics was the ruling party line that the country's wealth and strategic location made it a special target for the evil, potent forces of communism, with whom it was locked in a desperate battle for supremacy: regretably, this struggle sometimes required a temporary suspension of democratic processes and the rule of law. There was enough truth in the argument to make it plausible and partly mute criticism of questionable government actions, which the government in turn accepted as license to enact ever more draconian legislation. But sometimes not even the brutal apartheid laws were enough to silence dissenting voices or curb rebellious activities and then the regime's survival-at-all-costs mentality would drive it to solutions that inevitably led to the sudden disappearance or unfortunate death in custody of unyielding political activists. Official explanations of these deaths were as cynical as they were transparent: death by falling from a window; death by slipping in a shower; death by strangulation, from shoelaces, in a cell; death by strange encounter with a wall; death by unexplained injuries; death by falling off a bed; the causes were interchangeable but the results were always the same: the permanent removal of another thorn in the official hide.

Thabo had the sort of unbending demeanor that guaranteed he would likewise meet an untimely end should he ever fall into the tender clutches of the security police. He knew this, yet I never once saw him flinch or turn aside from circumstances that challenged him to face the white monolith head on. His commitment to the cause of black liberation in general and to the ANC in particular was total.

The African National Congress was formed in 1912 as a multiracial organization dedicated to the elimination of racial discrimination and the establishment of full voting rights for all South Africans. Although originally non-violent, the government in 1960 banned the ANC and in exile in neighboring Mozambique, they developed a military wing, Spear of the Nation, which engaged in sabotage and guerilla training. Four years later the ANC's most famous son, Nelson Mandela, was sentenced to life imprisonment for sabotage after being acquitted of treason at an earlier trial. Thoroughly demonized by the white government who labeled it a communist-inspired terrorist organization wholly dedicated to the violent overthrow of white rule, the ANC was feared and despised by most whites.

My feelings towards the ANC were ambiguous. While I was opposed to the use of violence as a political tool I had seen enough of the self-righteously blind brutality that came with the enforcement of apartheid to surmise that the government and its agents had thoroughly earned whatever they had coming to them. However, in my relationship with Thabo my focus was not the ANC and its objectives; I simply knew that in this remarkable young man I had found a soulmate with whom I could work to bring about effective changes in the economic and social circumstances that governed my small corner of the world. I never set out to be a hero or a revolutionary; my motivation was the more mundane success of my business and the assurance of a secure and comfortable life for my growing family.

Danielle was born in 1985. With the birth of Lauren in 1987, Linda and I moved into a spacious new home located on a quiet back street in one of the better parts of Ficksburg. Compared to the dismal accommodations just a few miles away in Meqeleng, it was a palace. I felt no guilt at the contrast, only in the knowledge that the residents of Meqeleng were barred from the enjoyment of similar conditions not by personal shortcomings but by virtue of their skin color. The notion was ever present with me that through my work with the chamber of commerce and my relationship with Thabo in particular, I could help to hasten the inevitable day when the only criteria for success was individual ability.

Thabo's ambitions mirrored my own, yet he was much more direct and ruthless in his approach, believing that the government had long since forfeited any claim to morality and any expectation of sweet reasonableness from its opponents by its intransigent determination to hold onto power at any cost. I believed he would use any means necessary to achieve his objectives, including violence, yet he had a strong pragmatic streak that usually expressed itself in a low-key response when others around him called for violent action.

He was also very patient. For the first two years of our relationship he kept me somewhat at arm's length and the content of our frequent discussions - usually conducted on a street corner in downtown Ficksburg - centered mainly on procedural matters relating to the organization of his "planning committee". I had no idea then that he was the head of the ANC in our area but simply assumed that he was establishing a power base to counter the dead hand of the toothless Administration Committee. Gradually, however, our discussions took on more substance and we would meet in the back room of a restaurant in Meqeleng or in my business office. Sometimes I would be told about abuse suffered by a black employee at the hands of his or her white employer and I would either be asked for background information on the white individual, or to intervene directly on behalf of the black employee. On other occasions the issue might be the abuse of police power: a child had been arrested and the parents could obtain no information about the whereabouts of their child or the nature of the charges against him. Or a relative had died in Lesotho and the family was unable to cut through the combined obstacles of red tape and official indifference to transport the body across the border for burial in Ficksburg.

As my involvement in these matters escalated my reputation spread through the black community as someone who could be trusted to intercede with white officialdom on their behalf and sometimes I would arrive at work in the morning to find a long line of petitioners outside my office. It could take several hours to process all of their requests and complaints and I would often call on Thabo to assist me. In this way our working relationship became very close even as our respect grew for each other. This was vital preparation for the perilous times that lay ahead. Towards the end of the 1980's the political impasse in South Africa was becoming intractable as demands from black citizens for justice and equality grew more strident and the government's response grew more heavy handed. Ficksburg was not immune to these currents and tensions there threatened to boil over early in 1989 when a black youth was shot and killed while resisting arrest after being caught shoplifting. I received an urgent call from Thabo to meet him in Meqeleng. Because there were few telephones in the black township and my personal and business telephones were in any event tapped by the security police, summonses from Thabo were always delivered in person by a trusted messenger.

He came straight to the point when I joined him an hour later.

"I want you to go to the police chief and find out if this shooting was accidental or deliberate. If it was deliberate the policeman responsible must be formally charged and answer for his actions in open court. Either way, we also need a formal public apology for the tragedy. Can you do this in a way that these people will listen to you?"

I nodded my assent even as I wondered how I would pull it off.

Then Thabo added: "Phillip, I want you to make them understand that if we don't get a suitable response there's going to be hell to pay. The whole township will rise up and march on Ficksburg."

Early the next morning I found myself sitting across the desk from Captain Theron, Ficksburg's police chief. He had reluctantly agreed to see me after I told him it was a matter of life and death. When I outlined the gist of Thabo's message the policeman reacted in a rage.

"Who the hell do you think you are to come into my office with these outrageous demands and threats?" he roared. "I want to know who's behind this and I want to warn you that you're playing a very dangerous game that is going to get you into a lot of trouble."

I had expected this response and I sat quiet and unblinking until the man exhausted his spleen and then glared at me in silence, waiting for my answer. I said nothing and the silence grew thick between us. Finally he pounded the desk with his fist and demanded: "Talk to me!"

Very quietly, looking him directly in the eye, I replied: "There's really not much more to say. I'm just passing a message on to you. You can chose to ignore it or you can waste time on chasing rabbits or you can do something positive. The ball's in your court."

A look of uneasy bemusement crossed the captain's face.

"Rabbits?"

"Yes. It doesn't matter where the message comes from or what my motivation is and if you chase those rabbits you'll get nowhere. What matters is that war might be about to break out in Ficksburg and you can stop it."

A glint of uncertainty in the man's eye encouraged me to lean towards him and add with deliberate emphasis: "The demands are not unreasonable. But if you ignore what I'm telling you, if you pass up this opportunity to avoid unnecessary violence and bloodshed, and the violence does come, I want to assure you that I will make public the fact that you knew about it in advance and you could have stopped it."

Now it was the police chief's turn to stare at me unblinking. I got up to leave. As a parting comment I said to him, "Perhaps you should check with your superiors about a suitable response."

The next morning Captain Theron called me to invite me back to his office. His demeanor was quite different from the day before and as he greeted me he indicated a fresh-faced but extremely nervous young policeman sitting in the corner.

"This is Constable Retief. He's the young man involved in the shooting and I want you to hear from his own mouth what he has to say."

I felt sorry for the constable. He looked like he was about to face a firing squad and his agitation and distress was palpable as he haltingly told his story. The gist of it was that he had responded to a complaint about a shoplifter and when he arrived on the scene the black youth had lunged at the pistol on his belt. In the ensuing struggle a shot was fired and the alleged thief lay dying with a bullet in his abdomen.

I had no doubt that Retief was telling the truth.

Captain Theron added that a full departmental investigation had been conducted and the constable had been exonerated of all blame.

"I also want you to know that the unfortunate parents will receive a letter from me expressing my regrets, and a similar statement will be issued to the local newspaper."

I warmly thanked the police chief for his gracious response and hastened to give Thabo the news. He looked relieved.

"You know, for a moment there I thought they were going to try and stare us down on this one. Phillip, you did a great job!"

Shortly thereafter I received a summons to meet Thabo and my guide directed me to a shebeen - an illegal drinking establishment secreted in the back part of a tiny Meqeleng house. My host was already there. When I walked in he produced a bottle of Johnny Walker Scotch whisky with a flourish and declared that it was time for us to relax a little together. There were several others present, some of whom I did not recognize.

"Don't worry," Thabo laughed as he caught my nervous glance around the room, "you're among friends. "Please, sit down. Relax. We've got this area cordoned off and nobody's going to disturb us here."

Again, I was made conscious of an invisible organization that somehow functioned efficiently despite the always-looming presence of police and security forces. I was often aware in a vague way of a hidden but tangible presence that seemed to surround me when I found myself in situations of potential danger, as when I would drive away from a meeting with Thabo after dark and sensed rather than saw the shadowy figures that tracked my passage on every street corner until I was safely home. I always took the precaution of using an unmarked beat-up old delivery van from my warehouse when I visited Meqeleng, rather than my big white Land Rover which was well known around town, but it was still risky moving in and out of an area that was off limits to whites.

Later, when my ANC membership was public knowledge, the threat came not only from the white authorities. The Pan African Congress, or PAC, was a radical group to the left of the ANC, committed to the violent overthrow of the government. They viewed the ANC as compromisers who preferred talking to action, and they launched frequent terrorist attacks on white farmers and the police with the sole aim of creating uncertainty and instability in the white community. Thabo one day casually explained to me that I was an inviting target for them because they resented the fact that my vice chairmanship of the ANC lent the organization enormous credibility in the black community. In answer to my expression of alarm he said to me in mock seriousness, "Hey, man, look at it this way - the bullet that finally gets you will be thoroughly democratic because it may come from a black hand or a white hand!"

I lamely thanked him for his unique insight.

But this night in the shebeen there was to be no talk of death or hardship or problems. It was just a fun time with a few friends gathered around a bottle of good whisky. As we drank our way through the first bottle and Thabo produced another, he regaled me with stories about the private lives of Ficksburg's white establishment.

"We've got a file on everybody whose anybody in this town," he declared. "Man, if they knew the things we know about them it would scare them half to death. You see, the way it works is that to the average white person us blacks are almost invisible. I mean, they don't actually think of us as people - thinking, feeling, hearing, and seeing people. We're just drones who do the work. So they'll do things and say things in front of us, and sometimes to us that expose them totally for what they are and who they are. It amazes me sometimes the information we get back from the maids and the waiters and the cooks and the cleaners and the caddies and the drivers who go about their jobs pretending to be dumb and blind while their white masters expose every little secret to them. I bet I know more about the Catholics in this town than the priest does who hears their confessions. In fact, I know more about the priest himself than anybody in his church does."

With this Thabo slapped his knee and grinned broadly as a memory came back to him. "Yes, sir, I know a lot about that old priest that his church would just love to know!"

Then serious for a moment he added, "But we're not in the sleaze business. Most of the information we get we discard because it's not useful to us. On the other hand, some of the information is very relevant and then we file it away for use on a rainy day."

I wondered to myself if possession of such information partly accounted for Thabo's seeming immunity from police harassment. Or perhaps direct payoffs to the police were the answer. I wasn't sure how these things would work and in any event this possibility would indicate that Thabo was hooked into some much larger organization. But I didn't want to engage in fruitless speculation. Some things were better not to know.

By now all of us were moderately drunk and there was a lot of laughter in that tiny room as we sat on our cheap plastic chairs and passed the bottle around to refill our never empty glasses. But, inevitably, the conversation struck a serious note. It was always this way in South Africa; beneath the levity, even on a sunny day, there was always pain. Somewhere towards the end of the second bottle a cloud passed over Thabo's face and he stared earnestly into my eyes.

"You know, Phillip, sometimes there are things I know that I don't want to know. Things that are too heavy. Things that are hard to believe, even here." He paused, as if weighing how much to share with me. Then he shrugged and said, "Hey. One day if we all live long enough the truth will come out. But I have been told by people I trust that the government, your white government, has formed a Chemical and Biological Warfare program for use against its political enemies. People in detention are injected with toxic chemicals. I've even been told that some are drugged and then dropped into the sea from aircraft. So what do you think about that, hey?"

I was appalled. It felt like someone had reached through my alcoholic haze and punched me in the stomach. I stared numbly back at Thabo and asked him, "I don't know what to believe. Why are you telling me this?"

"Because I want you to understand that we're not playing games," Thabo responded. "I don't know you well enough to know what motivates you, Phillip. I admire you and I'm grateful, very grateful, for the help you give us, but I want to be sure you understand that you're getting into some deep water here."

Ten years after this revelation, with the ANC firmly in power, I was sent a newspaper clipping to my home in the United States. It told about the trial of former senior officials of the apartheid regime who had waged a "dirty tricks" campaign in the 1980s and it substantially confirmed everything Thabo had told me. The news was no less shocking than the first time I heard it, in that little back room in Meqeleng. But back then I remember being oppressed by the dread feeling that I was participating in events that were already way beyond my ability to control or even anticipate.

Several weeks after our drinking session it was confirmed to me that Thabo was far more than a freelance agent with only an altruistic desire to help his fellow citizens. The unavoidable realization that I was dealing with the leader of a shadowy and very powerful organization whose reach extended far beyond Ficksburg came as a chilling shock and I wondered why I had made myself blind to this fact in the preceding years.

As usual, Thabo wasted no time in getting to the point as he visited me in my downtown office.

"We're planning a week-long boycott of Ficksburg. Nobody's going to turn up for work and nobody's going to spend a penny in the town until we announce that the boycott is over. It's time for us to flex our muscles and show who's really in charge here."

"Why are you doing this now," I asked, feeling it was prudent to forego the obvious question of whom he represented.

"Because the day is coming when we're going to be staring eyeball to eyeball with the government and when that happens we want them to know who they're dealing with. The boycott in Ficksburg will be part of a nationwide campaign."

A hollow feeling settled in the pit of my stomach as I realized I had just been made privy to information that could get me thrown in jail, or worse.

Thabo smiled as he saw my obvious discomfort.

"Hey, don't worry Phillip. This is where all our hard work of the last few years pays off. We're in the home stretch now and we're going to see some big things happen. It could get hairy at times but I want you to know we're going to protect you as much as we can."

I wasn't sure precisely what Thabo meant until the boycott was launched two weeks later. The promised protection was so overt as to be almost embarrassing. Ficksburg literally turned into a ghost town overnight, with every single business and public facility forced to close its doors either because of a total absence of workers or shoppers or both. Except my warehouse and two retail outlets. There it was business as usual as they remained open and fully staffed. In fact, it was more than business as usual as I did a roaring trade in the absence of any competition whatsoever.

Other business owners in the town were incensed, accusing me of collusion with the boycotters. My reply to them was simple.

"Perhaps your employees would be loyal to you and ignore the boycott too if you paid them better than starvation wages and treated them better than beasts of burden," I declared. But privately I knew there was more to it than that: no employee of mine would have dared to come to work without the permission and encouragement of Thabo and his "planning committee". In the same way, no black person would have dared to shop in one of my stores.

Later, Thabo declared the boycott a complete success as he explained the ANC's ongoing strategy to me. Although he had not formally announced to me his affiliation with the illegal organization he clearly assumed that I had drawn my own conclusions after the ANC claimed responsibility for the nationwide protest.

"We know we cannot win in an armed confrontation with the government," he said. "They've just got too much firepower on their side. But we've got numbers and time on our side and we're going to wear them down by constant civil disobedience and passive resistance until the country becomes ungovernable and the economy collapses. The outcome will be just the same as if we had a better trained army and a whole lot more bullets than they do."

The stakes began to escalate rapidly in the next few months. Inevitably, there was violence as passive resistance broke down or renegade individuals on both sides of the conflict deliberately sought open confrontation. I found myself in the thick of the action as leaders from both the black and white communities appealed to me to negotiate demands and counter demands on their behalf.

Sometimes I did not go home for days on end and the strain on Linda began to show. She was unaware of the details of what I was doing because I sought to protect her by telling her as little as possible about my political activities, but she knew enough to know that whenever there was turmoil in our community I somehow seemed to be near the center of it.

Then, in 1990, the unthinkable happened. Finally brought to its knees by stringent economic sanctions and the harsh demographic realities I had outlined to Ben Steyn many years before, the once invincible white government yielded to reality. In January the

128

ANC was unbanned and a month later Nelson Mandela was released after 27 years in prison.

I immediately approached Thabo and asked if I could formally become a card-carrying member of the ANC. Several weeks later he invited me to a meeting in Meqeleng.

"It's just a little gathering at the football stadium," he said.

When I arrived there I was mystified at the large crowd that had gathered. There must have been several thousand people present and I wondered why Thabo had not warned me in advance that something big was planned. For a moment the thought crossed my mind that perhaps Nelson Mandela was going to be present. As I walked into the stadium, the only white man in that vast throng, a tidal wave of chanting and ululating broke around me and the crowd parted in front of me as I was carried on a vast surge of noise and emotion towards the platform in the center of the field where Thabo stood beaming at me.

I was thrust onto the platform beside him and almost fell to my knees under the tangible weight of the thunderously swelling applause that was focused on that single spot. With a jolt of recognition more stunning than any electrical shock I realized in that moment that the applause was for me. I could not speak. I could hardly breathe. Tears ran unbidden down my cheeks and I finally turned to Thabo and buried my face in his shoulder.

At last the noise subsided.

"For the last five years you have stood beside us," Thabo said gently. "You have cared for us and helped us and risked your reputation and even your life for us.

129

In the process you have lost many of your white friends. But in their place you have gained these."

With that he waved his hand over the assembled throng and the applause broke out again. Then raising his voice to be heard above the noise he added, "This is our way of saying thank you."

Then he handed me my ANC membership card and announced to the delight of the crowd that I had been unanimously elected vice chairman of the executive committee.

Later that day I went home in a daze. When Linda asked me where I had been I simply told her that I was at a meeting. With a feeling approaching something like despair I recognized that there was not a white person in Ficksburg, not even my wife, who could possibly begin to understand or appreciate the tumultuous events of the last few hours and their huge significance to me. Indeed, as news of my ANC membership spread through the white community I was subjected to a crescendo of vilification during the next few days.

It wasn't long before the death threats started.

I remained strangely unmoved by it all. I had not felt particularly brave as a secret ANC sympathizer and I did not feel particularly scared now that my loyalties were exposed to shocked and angry fellow citizens who whispered darkly about retribution. As the months rolled by and the intensity of confrontations between black and white showed no signs of abating, it was pretty much business as usual for me in my role as mediator.

On the national political front there was increasing movement towards the establishment of a multi-racial government, a prospect that had been entirely unthinkable only a year before. But this happy development stood in stark contrast to the escalating turmoil in the country as the ANC kept up the pressure on the white government through strikes, boycotts and riots, while angry and confused whites lashed out at blacks or black sympathizers whom they felt had betrayed their cause.

It was during this dangerous period that I witnessed an act of raw courage that put all of my relatively poor efforts into their proper perspective. Not surprisingly, it involved Thabo.

Ficksburg was a center of right-wing extremism where the Afrikaner Weerstandsbeweeging - the Afrikaner Resistance Movement, or AWB - had a strong following. This uniformed neo-Nazi organization did much saber rattling in the months after Mandela's release, with rallies, marches and dire warnings of armed resistance if a black government ever came to power. Their warnings were given credence by the establishment of para-military training camps in various parts of the country, including Ficksburg, and the fact that they were always heavily armed. It was strongly suspected that the AWB enjoyed active support from right-wing elements within the government, police and the army, a suspicion that later proved to be true.

While the police were quick to respond to left-wing violence and enjoyed a high success-rate in the apprehension of suspected left-wing terrorists, they were strangely unable to come up with leads or to make arrests in response to increasingly frequent acts of right-wing violence - including the assassination of some prominent anti-government leaders.

It was against this background that the AWB announced it was going to hold an armed rally in Ficksburg as a show of strength and a warning to the ANC in the area that their resistance to the government would no longer go unopposed. Thabo immediately called me to a meeting.

"We can't let this go unchallenged," he said. "If those guys start strutting around town with their guns and we do nothing it will have a hugely intimidating effect on both blacks and whites here."

"What do you plan to do," I asked in alarm, with visions of outright-armed conflict dancing in my head.

"I'm going to attend their rally," Thabo said firmly.

I was aghast.

"You're crazy," I said. "If you get into the middle of that bunch you'll never come out alive. What's the point of throwing your life away like that?"

But Thabo was adamant. He said he planned to put his head right into the jaws of the lion to prove to his followers that it was toothless. The rally was planned for noon on the following Wednesday and he was confident that his security lay in confronting the AWB openly, in broad daylight and in the presence of many witnesses.

"And what if you're wrong?" I asked. "What if some crazed Nazi pulls a trigger and blows your brains out? What then?"

"Then you're going to have to make sure that the shooter gets arrested and thrown in jail," Thabo replied calmly. "This has to be one incident they don't get away with.

"I want you to stay in the background. If shooting starts and something bad happens to me it's essential that we have a live witness who is able to pick up the torch and ensure that justice is done. I plan to march on the Town Hall where they're holding the meeting. I don't think I'll have a big crowd with me because I'm going to let my people know the risks and ask only for volunteers.

"But I want you to stir as much uncertainty as you can amongst the officials in this town. Let them know that their every move is being watched and recorded so that the AWB sympathizers in their ranks understand they won't have a free ride if they turn violent. I also want you to lodge a formal protest with the Town Council over the fact that they've sanctioned this rally by allowing the use of the Town Hall. And then see if you can get any newspaper reporters to be there for the big day."

A week later as noon approached I found myself stationed in a strategic location at the bottom end of Ficksburg's main street, where it opened onto the large town-square. Half a dozen streets radiated from the square which was dominated by the solid stone structure of the Town Hall. All morning long truckloads of heavily armed, brown-uniformed AWB members had been arriving in the square, with the arrival of each truck greeted by roars of approval from the banner-waving crowd already present. The sinister blood-red AWB flag with its swastika-like emblem was everywhere. There was a strong police presence around the square and in the streets leading to it, but the police hung back and made no attempt to interfere. I was appalled by the size of the turnout. It looked like people were arriving from all over the country and I realized with an awful sense of despondency that the AWB leaders had decided to make a major statement here today: their movement was big, it was bold, it was tough and it had had enough of the government's weak-kneed sellout to communists and blacks.

Precisely at noon the assembled masses in the town-square began to file into the hall. It was difficult to estimate the size of the crowd but there must have been at least 500 present. Then my attention was caught by a stir several blocks up main street, away from the square, and I turned to see Thabo making his way down the street at the head of a small group. They walked quietly along the pavement and as they approached the square their numbers swelled from the addition of individuals who came out of the side streets to join them. By the time they reached the intersection opposite to where I was standing, there were about a hundred people with Thabo. He acknowledged my presence with a smile and then turned his attention to a police officer who had planted himself squarely in the middle of the street, blocking access to the square. They spoke for several minutes and then Thabo turned to me for help.

I made my way across the street towards him.

"What's the problem?" I asked.

"These people can't go any further," the policeman cut in. I recognized him as one of Captain Theron's lieutenants with whom I had had several encounters in the past.

"Why not?" I challenged him. "This is a public street and nobody here is causing any sort of disturbance. These people here have as much right to enter the square as those people over there," and I indicated the banner-waving, brown-suited ranks of the AWB.

A desperate look came into the policeman's eyes and I felt momentarily sorry for the man.

"Look," he appealed, "we don't want any trouble here. Why don't you just ask your friends to go home and let this meeting go ahead in peace? It will soon be over anyway."

By this time Thabo's supporters surrounded us and the policeman cast nervous glances over his shoulder as we continued our negotiations. Then there was a disturbance from the direction of the town hall and we all turned to determine its source. Incredibly, Thabo had used the cover of the milling crowd in the street to slip into the square with two or three of his followers and was approaching the entrance to the Town Hall. He looked so out of place there with his wild hair and a loud Hawaiin-type shirt that flapped around his compact frame, and I held my breath as I watched him saunter casually towards a group of AWB men who barred his way on the Town Hall steps. Beside me, I heard the policeman curse softly.

A pregnant silence descended on the square. Nobody moved, except the lone black man who had now reached the base of the steps. I wanted to weep and cheer at the same time. This incredible act of bravery was so blatant, so calculated, as to draw the grudging admiration of everyone who witnessed it, but my pride in Thabo's action was tempered by the horrified certainty that I would see him die in the next few seconds.

Then a figure separated itself from the AWB group at the top of the steps and came down to Thabo. I recognized the man as Eddie Von Maltitz, a virulent racist and local AWB leader who conducted frequent para-military training camps on his farm a few miles outside Ficksburg. He stood in front of Thabo and said something. Then he roughly pushed the black man backwards. Thabo smiled at him and made no effort to resist. His face contorted in rage, Von Maltitz drew his fist back to strike and as if on cue a group of policeman rushed forward and separated the two men. The angry voice of the AWB leader carried clearly across the stillness, hurling racial epithets against Thabo and cursing the police who restrained him. I watched in alarm as half a dozen policemen hustled Thabo across the street and into a waiting vehicle that gunned its engine and sped out of the square.

I guessed that they had taken him to police headquarters and quickly made my way there. I found Thabo seated in Captain Theron's office. He looked happy to see me.

"I'm trying to explain to the captain here that they've arrested the wrong man," Thabo said mildly.

I nodded my head in assent.

"I saw what happened. So did everyone else there. Von Maltitz assaulted this man without provocation. I want to lay a formal charge against him and I insist that you release Mr. Mokele immediately and arrest Von Maltitz instead."

Captain Theron sucked nervously on his bottom lip and drummed his fingers on the desk while I spoke. He remained silent for a long time and I was just about to repeat my statement when he gave me a level stare and addressed me slowly and deliberately.

"Mr. Thal, let's be honest with each other. This is not the time for posturing. You know perfectly well that if I try to arrest Von Maltitz we'll have a war on our hands. I don't want that and you don't want that."

Then turning to Thabo he added: "Mr. Mokele here is not under arrest. But I'm not going to release him either. I'm holding him here for his own safety until this whole unpleasant business goes away."

Thabo spoke up at this point.

"I insist that you let me go. You have no right to hold me here."

"And if I let you go, what will you do?" Theron enquired.

"I'll go straight back to that Town Hall and show that bastard I'm not scared of him," Thabo spat.

"Precisely!" the policeman replied. "Mr. Mokele, you're a brave man. A very brave man. But I can't let you go back there."

Incongruously, while this exchange was taking place I was mulling with some surprise the fact that it was the first time I had heard Thabo swear.

For the next several hours we continued our negotiations with Captain Theron, but he was unyielding. At one point he left the room in response to a telephone call and returned quickly with a worried look on his face.

"Mr. Thal, I need your help. Mr. Mokele's supporters are threatening to attack the Town Hall if they don't get an immediate assurance about his safety. I want you to speak to them."

I walked out of the police station onto the street and found half a dozen members of the executive committee there in angry debate with a group of police officers who looked relieved to see me. Calling the ANC men to one side I told them what was happening.

"What should we do?" they asked.

"I think the best thing to do is for everyone to head quietly back to Meqeleng," I replied. "We've made our point and I don't think further confrontation will serve any good purpose at this stage. Let's be thankful that nobody has been killed, and leave it at that."

When I got back to Thabo he gave me a withering look in answer to my recount of what had happened. For the first time since I had met him so many years before, I could tell he was angry with me.

"Phillip," he hissed, struggling to control his temper, "I want to remind you that I'm the chairman and I make the decisions. You're way out of line."

With that, he lapsed into silence. An awkward tension settled on the room and when Thabo was released several hours later we parted without speaking. He never referred to the incident again but when next we met I was aware of a certain reserve on his part.

Up to the time that I fled the country some two years after this event the breach between us was never fully healed. I was left to grieve for an extraordinary friendship that had been both forged and marred by the turmoil that was sundering the fabric of the very strange society where fate had planted us side by side. I recognized as I mulled over the circumstances of our relationship that Thabo and I were very different individuals with little in common outside of our political loyalties, yet I was aware also that both of our lives had been enriched by the intense connection that had been forced upon us. Like so much else in South Africa, our friendship left me with a bittersweet sense of both achievement and loss.

CHAPTER NINE
Fear

Fear can sometimes be a tangible thing, like a hard, cold stone lodged in the gut. I got to know fear well in the months leading up to my flight.

In the years since 1985 I had witnessed many extraordinary events, but none of them really touched the secret place inside me where I could retreat for safety when circumstances became overwhelming. I experienced strong emotions, yes, like the feeling I had when I watched Thabo walk towards what I thought was his certain death; or the time when I stumbled on a township lynching and watched in stunned horror as a group of black teenagers placed a gasoline-soaked car tire around the neck of a wretched young man and set it alight. The fact that I was later told he had been a police informant in no way eased the nightmares that plagued me for weeks afterwards.

Yet I remained strong in that special place deep within.

Then fear came to lodge inside me. It began on the protest march: Thabo and I at the head of 5,000 township residents marching to the administration offices at the bottom of the hill leading to Meqeleng, and paramilitary units everywhere, in trucks, on the roadside, atop armored cars, rifles aimed and menacing. I looked into the eyes of the men facing me, people I knew, people I had played golf with and drank a beer with, whose children were schooled where my children were schooled; I saw the look of angry contempt in their eyes and studied the fingers on the triggers, and I was afraid.

This was not an existential thing: it was present, physical. My knees trembled. My mouth was dry. Horror consumed me as vivid images of Sharpeville and similar police-instigated massacres played through my mind. I knew what these men confronting me were capable of when they felt their authority was challenged by the black hordes whose numbers they feared so greatly, and I knew that one misstep could unleash a hail of bullets through my yielding flesh.

Sometimes, in a detached sort of way, when one is secure and the sun is bright overhead and the birds sing, it is comfortable to speculate on the manner of one's death. But when the prospect of death is actual the indulgent thoughts flee and there is only fear. It takes a supreme act of will to walk the next step. And the next. The body cringes and tries to make itself a small target; the senses scream and the skin crawls. There is no respite.

Step by cruel step we reached the bottom of the hill and handed our list of grievances and demands through the barbed wire and then we walked back the way we came. The guns were behind us now, the threat was behind us now, and the giddy feeling of life thrumming through adrenaline-charged veins was a natural high more potent than any drug.

I promised myself I would never do anything like that again, so the next time fear came to me the circumstance was not of my choosing.

It began innocently enough with a telephone call from the police and a polite request for an interview while I was working alone at the office on a Saturday afternoon. By this time, the summer of '93, my instincts were acute and dread fear began rousing in the corners of my mind. I called Linda.

"The police want to talk to me. Sergeant Malherbe. He's just called and he's on his way. It's probably nothing special but if I'm not home for dinner I want you to call Captain Theron and let him know that you know I'm in police custody. Then call our friends - the Roberts and the Barkers and the Bruces' and tell them the same thing."

It was a horribly cruel thing to do to an anxious wife who had endured more than her fair share of blind torment, but I didn't have much time and this call to Linda was my ace in the hole. If I needed one. My instinct told me I did.

Sergeant Malherbe arrived at my office a few minutes later. He was a big man with a beefy red face and massive arms that ended in huge, stubby-fingered hands. We knew each other well from my numerous encounters with the police and he gave me a familiar smile as he greeted me. The he invited me out to his car.

"I've got something I want to show you," he said.

I accompanied him outside. The car was parked in an alley around the side of the building and alarm bells began to sound in my head. The street was deserted. As we approached his vehicle I saw somebody was in the back seat and a moment later I recognized a policeman we dubbed The Weasel because of the oily manner that accompanied his small frame and rat-like features.

"Get in," Sergeant Malherbe said casually.

I hesitated. "What do you want to show me?"

"It's not far. Get in. I'll take you there."

My curiosity piqued, I got into the front seat of the car beside the beefy sergeant. He gunned the engine and we turned into the street. We drove in silence for several minutes before I realized we were heading out of town. I was about to remark on this fact when Weasel spoke behind me.

"Mr. Thal, do you love kaffir women?"

"What?" The question was so crude and unexpected it startled me.

"Kaffir women. Do you love them? How many of them have you made love to?"

I turned my head to look at the man in the back seat. He was sitting almost directly behind me but out of the corner of my eye I could see the smirk on his face and the big service revolver lying in his lap. The car was accelerating now on the highway that led north to Johannesburg, 300 miles distant, and with a cold shock of recognition I knew I was trapped in the vehicle.

My first reaction was anger. I spat my answer back at him: "Why don't you tell me? You watch my every move so I'm sure you've been keeping score!"

The confidence he displayed with his next retort jangled my nerves. Ignoring my remark, he asked in a sibilant tone, "So what's it like? Do you enjoy black meat?"

Clearly, the man felt he was completely in control of the situation and was undoubtedly following a pre-planned script. I realized it was vital not to let him know he was rattling me. So I twisted my body around until I could look him square in the eye and turned the question back on him, using the nickname that I knew he hated.

"Actually, Weasel, from everything I've heard, you're the expert in that area. Perhaps you'd like to tell me and the sarge here how it tastes."

Beside me, Sergeant Malherbe chuckled as he nodded to his colleague.

"Hey, Gawie, he's got you there, man!"

This was clearly the good cop/bad cop routine and I reminded myself not to be taken in by Malherbe, even as he turned to me and apologized for the other's rudeness. I cut him short.

"Look, I don't know what game you guys are playing but I don't have time for it. Take me back to my office."

Malherbe grimaced.

"Hey, man, relax. Relax. Old Gawie here and me just want to get to know you a little better."

I cut him short again: "Perhaps you didn't hear me! Take me back to my office."

Now the sergeant looked grim and his voice took on a firmer tone.

"Well, now, we can't do that. Not right away. You see, there are a lot of things we have to talk about and it might take some time. Of course, if you decide to be as friendly as we are, this could be over very quickly."

Then with a jovial look on his face as if he had just remembered something rather funny that would lighten the tone of our conversation he glanced at his colleague in the back seat and said, "Gawie! Tell him about that kaffir we found last night."

Behind me, Weasel guffawed.

"It was the funniest thing! The guy had been taking a crap in the woods there near the train station and someone shot him right between the eyes. He fell

144

straight backwards. So when we find him the guy's lying on his back there with his pants down and his legs in the air and his eyes crossed. Man! I wish you could have seen it!"

The two policeman roared with laughter at their recollection of the comical sight.

"This is going to get really nasty," I thought to myself. "These two are capable of anything and I'm completely at their mercy."

Ignoring my silence, Malherbe turned to me with a broad grin and said with heavy significance, "You know what's the best part of the story? Whoever nailed that kaffir was a great shot. In the dark. From fifty yards away. And he gets him right between the eyes."

Despite my intense resolve to stay in control of my emotions and not let these two thugs intimidate me, the cold stone of fear began to settle into its little spot somewhere within my solar plexus. The car continued to eat up the miles away from Ficksburg. Where were they taking me? My mind raced through various scenarios until a single picture came to me all unbidden: John Vorster Square?

Anything was possible, and the jolt of that dreaded name prickled my skin with a cold sweat. Johannesburg's notorious police headquarters had seen more than its share of "accidental" deaths in custody and I wondered at my chances of survival if that was indeed the destination of this unhappy drive.

Several hours passed as the two policemen continued to pepper me with questions in a vain attempt to engage me in conversation. I remained non-committal in response to the various subjects they raised, unwilling to give them an opening that they could pursue. It was growing dark. I glanced at my watch and Malherbe responded to the subtle movement.

"Your wife and children are probably wondering where you are," he said with a note of commiseration in his voice. "Perhaps we should head home."

"Perhaps we should," I responded. Then I played my ace. It wasn't much but it was all I had. "By now my wife has called Captain Theron and a whole bunch of other people just to let them know that she knows I'm on a joy-ride with the famous Sergeant Malherbe. So they're probably all looking for us about now."

"Is that right?" the big man responded. There was a long silence and then he added, "Well, I was thinking about taking you home anyway."

With that, he hit the brakes and threw the car into a well-executed power turn that had us facing back to Ficksburg within seconds.

"Not bad, hey?" he grinned. "Come on, now, you can at least compliment me on that turn."

"Pretty good," I said grudgingly, still a little breathless from the adrenaline rush that the tire-squealing slide across the roadway had brought on.

Then I froze as I felt the hard cold steel of a revolver pressed gently behind my right ear. Weasel's breath was warm on the back of my neck as he whispered into the same ear: "Do you know what this is? Have you ever seen what this will do to the back of a man's head? It's not pretty."

Then the pressure behind my ear was suddenly withdrawn as Weasel reached across my shoulder and dropped the gun into my lap. I let out a yelp of surprise.

"Don't worry," he laughed, "it's not loaded."

"Have you ever used one of those?" Malherbe asked with a sideways glance at me.

I turned the gun over in my lap. "Not exactly like this one. But similar. Why?"

Malherbe ignored my question and proceeded on a new tack.

"You do know that by law the police or army can call you up at any time for service?"

I was mystified by where the conversation was leading.

"So what?"

"When you're called up you have to obey orders, right?"

I remained silent. Malherbe repeated the question.

"You have to obey orders, right?"

"Yes, okay, so what's the point?"

"The point is that when we get back to Ficksburg..." and then he paused to correct himself, with heavy emphasis, "...*if* we get back to Ficksburg you're going to have a job to do and we expect you to do it properly. You're going to have to use this gun."

From behind me Weasel chipped in with a comment. "You know, it's a funny thing, but a gun doesn't have a mind of its own. A gun will do what we make it do. A gun can kill one guy just as easily as another."

"Yes, that's right," Malherbe agreed. "A gun doesn't have a conscience. Take that gun there in your lap. It could kill you just as easily as it could kill someone else."

The unsubtle inference was so blatant that I marveled at the temerity of these men.

"So who do you want me to kill," I said, impatient to get the charade over with.

"Thabo."

I was aghast. "You must be kidding!" I blurted out.

"No, man, I'm serious," Malherbe said, suddenly all businesslike. "That guy's got to go. And you're the man to do it."

I chuckled bitterly as I shook my head. "I don't believe this. I just don't believe it. You two bozos should be put in a zoo along with whatever crazy son-of-a-bitch it was who came up with this scheme!"

Then for the second time that fateful day I felt cold steel pressed behind my ear and Weasel's soft voice speaking to me.

"That gun you got there isn't loaded," he whispered. "But this one is."

With that, I heard the hammer draw back, inches behind my head.

"I want you to think about this, but don't think too long," Weasel continued. "It's his life for your life."

The terror that I felt in that second drained all the strength out of me. I saw that the whole bizarre car journey to nowhere had been designed to lead up to this horrifying moment and I felt utterly helpless to resist. I thought of Linda and the kids. I thought of my parents, long dead. I heard the voice of my brother talking to me on the telephone, the concern apparent in his voice even across the thousands of miles that separated us, warning me that this day would come and asking me what price I would put on it.

I had known all along, too, that this day would come.

Taking a deep breath I said very quietly, "Pull the trigger."

"What?" Weasel's voice was startled.

"Pull the damn trigger," I said, louder this time. "Go on, do it. Let's get this over with."

The next seconds might have been hours. I sat absolutely still, my hands folded in my lap, my head slightly bowed, eyes closed. I was ready to die.

Then there was a slight easing of the pressure behind my ear and I heard Weasel's worried voice seeking guidance from his companion: "Sarge.?"

Malherbe remained silent.

Weasel repeated the question, more insistent now: "Sarge!"

At last the sergeant spoke. His voice was bitter, angry. "Put the gun away. This *kafferboettie* - nigger lover - isn't worth shooting."

The relief that flooded me was more exquisite than anything I had ever felt. I wanted to laugh and cry at the same time. Instead, I lifted my head and spoke to both of them at once: "You guys are losers. You're sick losers. And one day you're going to pay for this."

Weasel cursed me from the back seat. Malherbe said nothing. Nobody spoke for the remainder of the journey. It was close to midnight when the car pulled up in front of my house and I stepped out onto my familiar driveway. My legs felt stiff and a little weak as I made my way to the front door, not looking back. I fumbled with the key in the lock. My hands were shaking. At last the door swung open and I stepped inside. I was safe.

Linda came running as I leaned weakly against the wall, trying to contain my emotions. She clung to me as anger, fear, despair and joy washed over me in alternate waves.

"I didn't know what to do," Linda sobbed at last. Her words came in a rush. "I called everybody you told me to. I called Captain Theron at home and he seemed mystified by your message, but I told him anyway that if you weren't home by morning I was going to call the newspapers and tell them the police had abducted you. Then I called our friends and they all came over and the Roberts are still here. Oh, Phillip, I've been so worried. Not knowing is the worst thing. Where have you been? Are you okay?"

I smiled weakly at her and said, "I'm fine. I need a drink."

We sat and talked until sunrise. Our best friends, Tim and Evelyn Roberts, stayed for an hour until they were satisfied that I was in good shape. We had shared so much together and nothing much surprised them anymore about my often-eccentric behavior, but I was touched by their genuine concern that was evident on this occasion.

"That was a scary message you left Linda! When you didn't come home I started taking bets on where we would find your body, "said Tim in his usual cheerful fashion. "But none of these other cheapskates wanted to ante up!"

I was non-committal about what had happened. The whole experience was too raw for my jangled nerves to relive so soon, and in any event I was not sure it would be a good idea to give Linda all the details. So I simply said the police had questioned me about my ANC membership and my activities on both sides of the border.

"They had a lot of questions and I didn't have many answers and they were persistent as usual," I said. "Time passed in a hurry."

Then Linda and I were alone.

"This has been one of the worst nights of my life," she told me. Then looking directly at me, she added, "Phillip, what's going on? What are you up to? All of this mysterious coming and going is unsettling. You're always at meetings. Whenever there's some sort of political trouble in town you seem to be involved. And now the police are harassing you. Are you going to get us all killed because of your involvement with the ANC?"

I tried to reassure her but this time she would not be satisfied by my vague answers. So I tried a different tack.

"Listen, there are people, ordinary people like you and me, ordinary families like ours, and nobody gives a damn about them. Somebody has to care for them. That's all I'm doing."

It wasn't quite the whole story but it sounded good to me and I hoped Linda would think so too. She didn't.

In a small voice she simply said, "But what about us? What about me? What about your children? Sometimes it seems this is just a place where you eat and sleep and we're all strangers to you."

I was about to reply but she held up her hand.

"No, let me finish. I want you to try and understand how I feel. I'm not complaining about what you've done for the children and me. We have a beautiful home. You're kind and generous and I can't think of a single material thing we need. But, Phillip, a marriage,

151

a life, is about more than material things. If the children and I lose you, all of this other stuff is meaningless."

She was crying now. Softly. I could sense the deep emotion and genuine fear behind her words and with a start I realized how I had been neglecting my own family while trying to help others. Searching for the right words I said, "You know, I'm not even sure how this whole thing started. It's not as if I woke up one morning and decided I wanted to join the ANC. Sometimes I feel overwhelmed by it all.

"I saw a cartoon once where a woman tugged at a little loose thread on the sleeve of a sweater, and pretty soon the entire thing had unraveled into a big tangled ball at her feet. That's me."

Linda smiled at the mental picture and I reached out to take her hand.

"Look, I've never seen myself as a hero or an activist. You know I don't like those people because they always look so self-important, so pleased with themselves. I just wanted to reach out and help somebody, and now sometimes I feel like I'm drowning. But I can't quit now; I can't walk away from what I'm doing, as if it was never that important. I have to see it through to the end. And I'm convinced the end will come soon."

"Yes, with a bullet in the head." Linda said bitterly. She did not know specifically what danger I was in but she did watch the evening news and it seemed hardly a day went by without reports of political violence in some part of the country.

"No! No!" I protested. "I really feel we're getting to the point where things will start to improve. Once we have a multi-racial government in power and people realize it's not the end of the world, this craziness will stop. You'll see. Things will get better."

I was wrong, yet I think I believed it at the time. I wanted to believe it.

But my optimism did not translate into reality and the fabric of our lives unraveled steadily in the months ahead as the violence and the harassment and intimidation increased. Sometimes the intimidation was so crude as to be almost comical.

A few days after my involuntary joyride to nowhere a police lieutenant visited us at our home. His sugary solicitude was so obviously forced that both Linda and I struggled to keep straight faces as he enquired after our health.

"I just want you to know that a lot of people in our town are worried about you and your family," Mr. Thal. "We don't want to see you hurt, but you know we can't protect you all the time and some of the people you have been dealing with are…unreliable."

"Oh?" I replied. "What people?"

"Um, the…the ah…the black people you've been dealing with."

"Oh, you mean the other members of the legal political party that I'm a member of? Do you mean the ANC, the same party that our government is negotiating with about multi-racial elections? Do you mean the ANC is unreliable?"

The lieutenant squirmed.

"Mr. Thal, I haven't come here to argue with you. I just want you to know that your friends are concerned about you."

"My friends haven't said anything to me. Do I have friends here I don't know about?"

"Well, you know, we're all your friends."

"Are you my friend?" I shot at the lieutenant, looking him directly in the eye.

He was momentarily nonplussed.

"Well, uh, yes. Yes, of course," he replied at last.

"Is Captain Theron my friend?"

"Yes, I believe he is."

"Then tell him to fire those two bastards who picked me up the other night and took me almost all the way to Johannesburg while they tried to convince me just how friendly they were," I snarled at him.

After the man left Linda turned on me and said, "You didn't tell me anything about a car ride to Johannesburg. Just what did happen that night?"

"Oh, it was nothing," I replied.

But Linda knew I was lying. Finally, she took matters into her own hands by announcing that she and the children were going to stay with friends in Cape Town for a few weeks.

"I feel like the whole world is closing in on me. I've got to get away," she said.

I agreed to her going with mixed feelings, wondering if she would ever come back. Two days after she left with the children a molotov cocktail was thrown into our yard and I took it as a fortunate omen that she was not at home at the time. The small and crude firebomb did little damage and I said nothing to Linda about it, but she heard the details from our terrified maids shortly after her return.

Nevertheless, she told me she was back to stay. "I'm probably crazy, but you're my husband and I love you and my place is here beside you," she explained.

Then the phone calls started. Every night between the hours of one a.m. and four a.m. the phone would ring and a heavily accented voice would repeat the same sinister message: "It's time to wake up because we're on our way to kill you."

My response would always be the same - a single crude phrase about the caller's ancestry before dropping the phone back into its cradle beside my bed. Then I would turn over and go right back to sleep.

Linda was appalled at my casual attitude but I explained to her that if the person behind the threats really intended to come over to our house and kill us all in our beds the last thing he would do would be to warn us in advance so that we'd be waiting for him. To aid her sense of security, however, I bought a small arsenal of weapons and taught her how to use them. Each night as we went to bed the last thing we did before turning out the lights was to lock and load pistols that we kept close to hand on our bedside tables. Downstairs in my study were a fully loaded semi-automatic shotgun and several high-powered rifles. The safe in the study contained 1,000 rounds of ammunition for each weapon. I was ready for war.

Linda and I worked out a detailed plan of defense if ever our home was attacked. We also decided it would be prudent to train the children so we patiently coached six-year-old Lauren and eight-year-old Danielle about what to do if bullets were fired at the house.

At about the same time I began to carry a pistol in my belt whenever I left the house and I had another gun in the draw of my desk at the office.

Then John Craig died.

The media was full of the story because the official version had it that he had been assassinated by the ANC. Pundits of all stripes were quick to opine on the basis of this news that blacks could not be trusted and well-meaning but sadly deluded white supporters of the ANC, like myself and John, would sooner or later pay a high price for our folly. The scenario was just too convenient for our enemies and I said so, in public and in private. But with no facts to go on it was difficult to counter these arguments and the suspicions of John's brothers and their grieving parents. The tension between David and I - John's older brother and my business partner - became acute.

To add to the pressure on me I was confronted in the street outside my office the next day by an off-duty policeman who said he sympathized with me over my friend's assassination.

"The ANC never killed him," I said vehemently.

"Perhaps," the man replied coolly. "But have you thought about the fact that whoever did it might come after you next?"

"Let them come!" I said, angry at the blatant threat. "I'm ready."

"Perhaps," the policeman repeated, eyeing the pistol on my hip. Then with an icy tone in his voice he looked me directly in the eye and said, "I can see you've taken precautions to protect yourself. But you know, Phillip, it's very hard to protect your children 24 hours a day."

With that he turned and walked off. I was left standing on the sidewalk, suddenly cold in the sunlight, paralyzed by the conflicting tensions of roiling anger and impotence. For a brief moment I put my hand on my pistol and thought about shooting the man in the back as he casually strolled away from me.

Then I called Linda at home.

"Where are the children?"

"At school of course." There was puzzlement in her voice. "Is anything wrong?"

"No. Nothing's wrong. Be sure to pick them up in your car after school and bring them home."

Now the fear was evident in Linda's voice. "Phillip, what's going on? You know the school is only one block from our house. Tell me what's happening?"

"Nothing's happening. It's okay. I just think with all the craziness going on we should keep a closer eye on them. Don't let them out of your sight any more."

48 hours after the news broke about John's death Thabo was able to give me the complete details of what happened. In all my years in South Africa I was never able to fully comprehend the workings of the incredible "bush telegraph" that sped information among the black community sometimes at greater speed and with more reliability than conventional, western forms of communication. Going right back to my childhood years when my parents were always informed about my safety as I rode alone in the Lesotho mountains, I had been aware of this hidden communications web. I had seen it work on those occasions when our heavily laden trucks became bogged down during a river crossing. Inevitably, a blanketed rider would come along and we would ask

him to get a message to the nearest village with a team of oxen to pull us out. He would amble his pony to the top of a nearby rise and call out the message. Somewhere nearby a group of women at work in a field would hear the message and pass it on. And so it would travel from hilltop to hamlet to field to hilltop until it reached the right ears, usually within a very short space of time, and soon the oxen would arrive. The system never failed.

With this rapid communication also came a general awareness among the black community about the true state of affairs in the country. I saw this demonstrated in a dramatic way that affected me personally when one day I traveled to a yacht race on the huge Vaal Dam near Johannesburg, about 300 miles from Ficksburg. It was 1993, the year my crew and I won the South African Championionships in the Stadt 23 Class, and a few months before John's death. Yachting gave me a welcome respite from the pressures I was under and I had resolved to maintain a low political profile among my yachting friends, so nobody in this area, so far from my small hometown, was aware of my political activities and my ANC membership. Or so I thought.

On the day of the race I pulled my yacht up to the slipway where a team of black men employed by the race organizers was manhandling yachts into the water. There was a huge traffic jam of trucks, boats and trailers and the launching team was doing an efficient but slow job of working their way through the mess. My yacht was towards the back of the line and it looked like I would have a wait of an hour or two ahead of me, so I decided to walk up to the clubhouse for a beer. As I passed by the head of the line I said a friendly hello to some of the black men working there, whom I had met briefly on previous visits to this place. A short time later as I sat in the clubhouse enjoying my first beer, I received a message to return to the river because my yacht was in the water. Mystified, I made my way down to the water's edge, certain that there was some mistake. As I approached the slipway I became aware of the cold stares of my fellow yachtsmen. A small knot of them in angry debate with the launching crew turned on me.

"This isn't very good form, you know," said one of them.

"What do you mean?" I asked, completely in the dark as to what had happened.

"I mean that you got these muntu's to launch your boat ahead of everyone else. I don't know how much you paid them but you should have been satisfied to wait in line like the rest of us."

I was mortified. "There must be some misunderstanding," I said. "I'm terribly sorry. I have no idea what happened here. In fact, I was in the clubhouse enjoying a beer because I though it would be more than an hour before my boat was ready."

Later, when the fuss had died down and all the boats were in the water the leader of the work crew came over to me. "I'm sorry, boss, that these other people were angry," he said. "But we know who you are and when you come here your boat must always go in first."

I was stunned. The man was clearly alluding to my ANC involvement although I had never mentioned it to him. I barely knew him. And when I responded that I was perfectly happy to take my place in line like every one else, he repeated adamantly, "You must always be first. When I work here you must always be first."

I saw it was pointless to argue with him and instead shook his hand, thanking him for his consideration. He looked very pleased.

Now here I was several months later being briefed by Thabo whose information had come through the same mysterious system. "It was an ANC comrade who shot your friend," he announced, carefully studying my reaction. I made no comment. "I'm sorry, Phillip. That part at least is true."

"Go on."

"The police had nabbed him in a raid about a week earlier. They found an AK47 with him. The guy was careless and they got him. He knew he was a dead man; the only remaining question was, how was he going to die. I guess the police interrogator did a pretty good job of convincing him it would be very unpleasant, because when they offered him his life back he agreed.

"They gave him a gun. They told him the target was John Craig. They gave him three days to get the job done and then they would come after him. But if he was successful they would tear up the file on him and he could disappear.

"So the guy turns up on Mr. Craig's farm and asks to buy some milk. When his target turns his back on him, he puts a bullet into the back of his head. He was positively identified by several people at the scene."

"Where is the shooter now?" I asked.

"He's disappeared. But we'll find him. In the meantime you should also know that the stories about a weapon and money being stolen at the scene are untrue. The security police are simply trying to establish a plausible motive for the killing, to show that the ANC is just a grubby little band of untrustworthy kaffirs."

Later that same day I passed the news on to David. He did not seem to believe me.

"The fact is, if you had never encouraged John to join the ANC he would still be alive today," my friend said bitterly.

"David, you know that's not true," I answered him, keeping my voice level. I had no wish for acrimony at a time like this. "John may have been your little brother but he was very different from you and the rest of the family. He wanted to make a difference and he saw his membership of the ANC as a positive step in that direction. Which I believe it was."

"Yeah. And now he's dead!" David looked at me with real hostility in his eyes and added, "I don't want to talk about it any more, Perhaps you should go now."

I drove home with tears in my eyes.

I had first met John about ten years previously when he joined David and I on a fishing trip. He was in his early twenties, big and robust and full of life. Sensitive eyes stared quizzically at you from out of a handsome face and his ready laugh was as expansive as the great outdoors.

But what really struck me about John was that he brought his dog and his black nanny with him. She was an elderly and very dignified Xhosa woman who immediately took charge of the small cottage where David and I had been living on our own for three days. She demanded that the three men present clean the place, announcing loudly that she refused to live in a pigsty. Both John and David spoke her language fluently and immediately obeyed. I was mystified by the exchange and turned to David: "What's up?"

"We have to clean up here," David mumbled as he shot me a warning glance. I turned to see the nanny, hands on hips, giving me a withering stare and decided I had better comply. As I did I muttered to myself, "This is a totally insane country!"

A few minutes later the old woman emerged from the bathroom and spoke to David again. He walked from the room.

"Where are you going?" I asked.

"To bath. She says I stink." Then he looked over his shoulder at me. "And you're next!"

I learned later that the nanny's name was Esther but that she would only be addressed as Nonna. She had raised both boys since birth and after David married she became John's inseparable shadow, declaring that he was far too weak and foolish to care for himself. This was hard to believe of someone who stood well over six feet tall and was a world class polo player, but to Nonna he was still a little boy who required her close attention.

When John was married several years later Nonna died shortly after. Her work was done.

The next time I met him was on his farm several hundred miles from Ficksburg, on the other side of Lesotho. His beautiful wife, Betty, was a vivacious blond and they had three small children. John had invited me to the farm to show me what he was doing for his black laborers. It was unlike anything I had seen before.

Traditionally, laborers lived on white farms in their own little mud huts and scratched a subsistence living from a small patch of ground for which they offered their toil to the farmer in exchange. It was a feudal system that had died out in Europe centuries before but was still very much alive in Africa. John decided he would get much better results if he partnered with his laborers, without whom the farm could not survive in any event, and so he built them a model village with modest but comfortable cottages that enjoyed the unheard of amenities of electricity and running water.

We talked long into the night about the South Africa we were inheriting from our fathers and found that we both shared a deep-seated antipathy for the mean prejudice and self-righteous myopia of most whites, especially those who supported the government and its oppressive policies with a smug religious fervor.

With a glint in his eye John told me, "Phillip, here on this farm I believe I can show there is a better way."

We spoke several times in the following months as John plumbed my political views. Immediately after the ANC was unbanned he called to ask me how he could join.

I remembered thinking later, as I meditated on his death, how the apartheid monster had again devoured one of the country's best and brightest, and how impoverished we were becoming.

About a week after John's death I woke to find that someone had spray-painted my double garage doors with the crude phrase, "kaffer lover."

A few day's later shots were fired at the house as we slept.

I was woken by the sound of glass splintering in the kitchen downstairs. Seconds later I heard the spiteful sound of another rifle shot and the dull smack of a bullet hitting a brick wall. Linda was already awake and both of us slid simultaneously to the floor, grabbing our pistols from the bedside tables as we did so. While she crawled to the children's bedroom to hustle them into the relative safety of the passage, I made my cautious way downstairs.

I had practiced this drill many times before, with my eyes closed so that I could find my way around easily in the dark. First I crept to the place where I had my loaded automatic shotgun hidden, and then did a cautious circuit of the downstairs area until I was satisfied that nobody was in the house. I knew that Linda wouldn't move from her position with the children until she got the all clear from me.

My dominant emotion was anger, rather than fear. I was confident that if I did encounter someone, or even several people, the brutally effective weapon in my hand would outgun them. At close range it was absolutely devastating and anybody who confronted me was in for a very rude surprise. But the house was empty and I called Linda downstairs. The noise we had heard from the kitchen was the sound of several glass vases shattering on the floor after they were knocked from the windowsill by the entry of a bullet. There was a neat hole in the window and on the brick wall opposite the window was an ugly depression caused by the bullet's impact. By the size and shape of the hole it was clear that a high-powered rifle had been used. Later the next day I discovered a second bullet hole in the outside wall beside the kitchen window.

Linda and I debated whether we should report the incident to the police. It was just as likely they had fired the shots as anyone else, but the decision was made for us when a squad car arrived about half an hour later.

"You neighbor reported shots being fired," the two policemen told us.

"Which neighbor?" I asked.

"I am not at liberty to divulge that information," the senior of the two said to us with solemn formality.

"Hey, I just want to thank the guy," I said. But I knew that Ben Steyn, my closest neighbor was away at the time and I doubted that the people on the other side of me would have heard the shots because of the way our houses were situated.

The policemen laboriously took our statements and then left, but not before darkly warning us that we should ask for police protection. I made it clear to them that we were well able to protect ourselves.

But after this incident there was an almost constant police presence across the road from our front door. Linda and I knew it was less for protection than to monitor our every move. I tested this theory by telephoning some friends and inviting them to a special ANC meeting at our house. I knew my telephone was tapped and within half an hour there were three police vehicles in view.

Drink in hand I walked into the street and waved at them. They did not wave back.

"They just sit there!" Linda screamed one day as she glared out of the window at the single vehicle present. "Like a bunch of zombies. Zombie vultures!"

The pressure was taking its toll. Days sometimes passed with Linda and I hardly speaking to each other. I could feel her burning resentment at the intolerable situation in which we found ourselves because of my political affiliations. Sometimes I woke in the middle of the night with the weird feeling that a huge wall of water was building behind the ceiling above my head and it would soon engulf me.

Then late one night as I sat downstairs in the darkened house, grateful for the solitude, the telephone rang.

"Probably another crank call," I thought.

The voice on the other end of the phone was strained, hushed: "Phillip? Listen, I'm only going to say this once…"

CHAPTER TEN
Albuquerque

The unpronounceable name wasn't the only thing that struck us as strange about our new home. Everything we encountered in those first few tentative and insecure weeks was different, foreign, sometimes even threatening. The hangover of fear did not go easily.

On our second day in Albuquerque the horror of what we had left behind us was made starkly evident to my brother. He had come to check on us in the evening on his way home from work, and as we sat and talked in our small, sparsely-furnished livingroom Danielle was playing a few feet away in the kitchen, bouncing up and down on a brightly colored beachball Linda had bought for her earlier that day.

Without warning, the ball popped, making a surprisingly loud bang. Linda, the children and I all dived to the floor. The two girls immediately snaked their way across to the outer wall of the apartment, under the main window, and huddled there. My brother was left standing alone in the center of the room, his mouth open.

"What on earth is going on?" he demanded, a look of stunned confusion on his face.

Sheepishly, as Linda comforted the children, I explained that back in South Africa we had so often practiced what to do in case our home came under attack that we had reacted instinctively to the noise of the ball popping. Our house there was a solid brick structure and the drill was to dive below window level at the sound of the first bullet. In addition, the children

167

were trained to crawl immediately to the outer wall of the house, beneath a window, because that was the safest place to escape whatever it was that might come in through the window.

As understanding dawned my brother reacted angrily. "I can't believe you lived under these conditions! How could you have subjected your family to this? What were you thinking?"

"It's not as if I chose this lifestyle," I lashed back at him.

"No, but you could have left a whole lot sooner, before things got this bad," my brother retorted. "It's absolutely insane that you continued to live there like frightened animals."

He was shouting now and I appealed to him for calm.

"Listen," I said, "us fighting isn't good for the kids either. The point is, we're here now, and we're safe, so let's just be grateful for that."

Not that we felt entirely safe; at least, not for a while.

Crowded supermarkets and shopping centers were particularly unsettling because they were such ideal targets for terrorist bombs. It took a real act of will for Linda and I to go shopping during the day, when the crowds were greatest. We had to constantly remind ourselves that South Africa was a long way away. But for the first week or two it was easier to simply shop late at night.

It was equally unsettling when perfect strangers looked us directly in the eye and offered a cheery, "Hi! Howya doing?"

When you know your life is in danger it is safer to remain anonymous. In particular, never talk to strangers because their motives are always suspect. So the procedure we learned was instinctively to isolate ourselves from those whom we did not know well. We would avert our gaze, turn away or back off whenever we felt uncomfortable in the presence of a stranger, which was often. It was only after several weeks in Albuquerque that we began to understand fully how aberrant our behavior was; how weird we must have seemed to Americans whose natural instinct, fed by their great freedom and sense of complete security, is to reach out in a friendly way to others, especially, it seemed, to strangers.

On a somewhat lighter note was the problem of multiple choice we encountered when shopping. We would be simply overwhelmed by the impossibility of making a selection from ten different types of baked beans or an entire aisle full of bread in every variety imaginable - and some beyond imagination - or the complexity of picking out something as simple as a dishcloth from scores of different colors, sizes, textures and prices. We had lived a wealthy lifestyle in South Africa and felt that we had lacked for nothing in the way of material comforts, but that was partly because we did not know what we were missing! America was a land of plenty and excess where the slightest whim was catered to. You only had to wish it and you could have it. Sometimes even before you wished it somebody else had decided you needed to have it.

And then there was the quite overwhelming kindness we experienced. Kindness and generosity were not invented in America, they've just become an

169

art form here. Everyone we met was genuinely, touchingly interested in us and concerned for us. This was demonstrated in the most powerful way to our children. When we fled South Africa, Lauren and Danielle were told they could only bring one toy each with them. After days of agonizing indecision, Lauren selected her favorite teddy bear while her older sister chose a kiddy computer - a mini learning center that contained her favorite word and number games. A few days after enrolling the children in the school that was within walking distance of our apartment, we were asked to pick up some stuff for the girls.

Mystified as to what it could be, Linda and I turned up at the school together. There we found piles and piles of toys for the children, donated by their new school friends and teachers. Our whole family was stunned at such generosity.

The fact that the children were being formally educated at all was remarkable to us. Enrolling them had been as simple as arriving at the school one morning, a week after we came to Albuquerque, and introducing ourselves to the administrator. We expected to encounter a lot of objections, and delays in the form of red tape, not to mention considerable expense. Instead, we were told that the children had a right to be educated - and that was that.

The matter of our "rights" was a mystery that took some getting used to. The extraordinary truth that finally dawned on us was that as political refugees in America, with no formal resident status, we had more rights and constitutional protections than we ever had enjoyed as citizens of our own country. This awareness left us at once overwhelmed by gratitude for the safe haven we had reached, yet mourning for the impoverished society we had left behind us. It was the difference between living in a mature democracy and a police state.

Tragically, I had never felt completely at home in South Africa, partly because of my hostility towards the ruling party and partly because of my sense of guilt over the fact that so many of my fellow citizens were deprived of basic rights that I enjoyed simply because I wore a white skin. For the same reason I found it difficult to respect my fellow white South Africans. Even those who were not overt government supporters were perfectly happy to accept without question all the privileges that their race conferred upon them.

By contrast, I enjoyed the many expressions of patriotism I saw in America and felt drawn to participate because it seemed that the good things we enjoy here have been earned in a co-operative effort by all citizens.

Thus it was a shock to me when my brother expressed a contrary view, declaring that a significant number of citizens were at best cynically dismissive and at worst bitterly disdainful of all things American. What began as a casual conversation during those early days in Albuquerque soon turned into a heated argument that, up to the present time, has still not been fully resolved between us. Our different experiences of America have apparently given us a significantly different perspective on the social and political undercurrents that shape this nation.

Much of my focus during my time here had been on healing the psychic wounds suffered by my family and myself from the trauma of our latter years in South

Africa and our subsequent flight. And the sheer emotional energy expended in confirming our resident status here has left little time or inclination for much else.

Fortunately, we were aided in this process by an extraordinary stroke of good fortune that illustrated just how small the world really is.

In 1890, a little over one hundred years before our arrival in the United States, three brothers had left their ancestral home in Bernkastel, Germany, to seek their fortune. Two of the brothers came to settle on the wide-open South Dakota prairie that was yielding to a new wave of immigrant expansion. The third brother, my grandfather, settled in South Africa. All three brothers became successful farmers.

In 1990 my older brother arrived in Minneapolis, Minnesota, to take up a job as marketing vice president of an international management consultancy. Shortly thereafter he met his namesake, Steven Thal, who lived in the same city. As the two men swapped notes and referred to the intensely detailed family tree that Steven was constructing as a hobby, it transpired that they were cousins. From opposite ends of the world, where they had grown in very different circumstances, and through the passage of 100 years, two branches of the family had been reunited. The fact that my brother had by chance settled in the city where Steven lived made the reunion all the more remarkable.

But from my point of view the truly fortuitous aspect of this extraordinary reunion was the fact that Steven is a successful and highly respected Immigration Attorney. It seemed that fate was conspiring in every way to help us, for without his generous help, encouragement and guidance my later application for political asylum in the United States would have been a confusing and very expensive nightmare.

CHAPTER ELEVEN
El Paso

Uncertainty is the worst thing. Whether it is the uncertainty of not knowing when a lethal bullet may come, or the uncertainty of not knowing where you will make your bed in the next 24 hours, it is uncertainty itself, not the thing feared, that is finally the most difficult to bear. Uncertainty is a form of death because it makes your life pale. In the end it drives you to a sort of desperate fatalism that invites a man holding a gun to your head to pull the trigger.

There were days after our arrival in the United States when I was simply thankful to be alive, to rejoice in the exquisite feeling that today, here, now, I am free. And there were days when the hopelessness of my situation overwhelmed me and consumed me with guilt for exposing my family to terrible danger and the disruption of the orderly processes of life; the little, vital things that are not missed until they are gone: pets, friends, favorite places, nostalgic sounds, familiar smells, the comfortable fabric of home. Our successful entry into America ensured that violent death was no longer an immediate prospect, but it was only the first uncertain step in a lengthy and tedious search for life.

We filed our appeal for political asylum five months after our arrival, by way of a formal petition to the United States Government. At that instant our status changed from tourists legally here on visas good for one year, to asylees subject to deportation from the country on 24-hour notice. The threat of deportation was a chilling reality that fuelled our nightmares for the next 18 months. This waiting period was in some ways worse than the preceding years leading up to our flight from South Africa.

At the beginning of the 21st century there were at least 16 million refugees somewhere in the world. Around 10,000 of those try to find refuge in the United States each year. But many of the applications for asylum are either fraudulent or insubstantial and only one in every 200 is granted. The official definition of a refugee is someone who is afraid to go home for fear of persecution on account of race, religion, nationality, and membership in a particular social group, or political opinion. In order to gain asylum in the United States individuals must provide credible proof that they have suffered past persecution or have a "well-founded fear" of future persecution. It is not a scientific process. Officials of the Immigration and Naturalization Service conduct interviews at regional centers around the country and they must make determinations based on the evidence presented to them. In a very real sense they may be dispensers of life or death as they weigh the evidence to decide if the person seated opposite them is being truthful in his or her account of torments suffered at home, or is simply seeking a free ride into the United States.

El Paso, Texas, was the regional center where our fate would be decided.

The process as we experienced it was mundane in its details but each step was vitally important to establish the credibility of our asylum petition. After we completed a formal affidavit declaring our intent to seek asylum and outlining in detail the reasons why, the Immigration and Naturalization Service responded that our petition was not frivolous and entitled us to an asylum hearing. Crossing this all-important hurdle brought authorization to find work in the United States so that we could support ourselves at least until the process had run its full course. If at the end of the process our application was successful we would be able to apply for permanent residence that in turn entitled us to apply for citizenship. If our application was denied, our work status would not matter. Nothing would matter. Within 24 hours we would be placed on an aircraft back to South Africa.

But in the meantime we could work! Linda found a minimum-wage job at a pizza parlor. My work status changed from part owner and chief executive of a multi-million dollar corporation, to car salesman. Nobody wanted to offer meaningful employment to people whose legal status and residence status was uncertain, with no credit history and no previous employment references. But we found work, and we were grateful for it. Moreover, the children were happily settled into their new school and life had taken on a predictable pattern where immediate physical danger was not a concern.

Our style of life remained a far cry from what we were accustomed to, but we saw no need to complain beyond the small irritations that nipped at the heels of everyday living. These irritations revolved around questions of our identity and where we would be tomorrow. When people recognized our foreign accents and asked us where our home was, we were never quite sure how to respond. Where was our home? And when we went shopping, every purchase had to be weighed against the question, "If we are forced to leave tomorrow, can we take this with us?"

If the answer was no, there did not seem to be much point in buying the thing. So for our entertainment at home we bought a tiny transistor radio instead of the TV set we would have liked. Our furniture, such as it was, was rented. The old car I bought would not normally have been my first choice, or even my third choice, but it was good enough to get us to California for a brief vacation. At last we kept the promise to our children and showed them Disneyland.

Then I was on my way to El Paso for an interview with an immigration attorney Steven had referred me to. As it turned out this would be the first of nine visits to El Paso, each one a ten-hour round trip through the heat-blasted yet starkly beautiful New Mexico desert, loosely tracking the course of the Rio Grande until it led the way through the dry, sprawling Texas border town. On one side of the river is America; on the other side, so close as to be within hailing distance, is Mexico. Each time I entered the city on the highway that parallels the narrow river at this point I would look across at the modest shacks lining dusty roads that probe like arthritic fingers through the low-rolling brown hills and wonder at the people living there. How did it feel to be so close to America, land of plenty, land of promise; yet so far? I believed I knew.

My second visit to El Paso was for my INS interview. It was not necessary for Linda and the children to be present because I was the petitioner. My fate would be their fate.

The Immigration and Naturalization Service headquarters on Hawkins Avenue, near the airport, is a large building with a pseudo-classical facade that incongruously trumpets its official identity amidst the southwestern style architecture of its surroundings. Like INS offices everywhere bored yet not unfriendly officials who deal with long lines of anxious seekers after the American dream characterize it. Most of the people coming here each day would be seeking permanent residence status or work authorization; asylum seekers were relatively rare and when they did make an appearance they would most likely be from South American countries. More than once I was told that the nature of my case and the location of my home country were unusual.

The interview itself took place in a small room on the third floor. The only people present were myself, a representative from my lawyer's office, and the INS official, a soft-spoken middle-aged woman with a neutral demeanor.

"Just tell me your story, from the beginning, and please stick to the facts," the woman invited me after our introductions were complete. It sounded like she had spoken that phrase a thousand times before. The interview lasted two hours, substantially following the outline of the affidavit I had previously submitted. The six-page document told the story of my political activities in South Africa and the threats and harassment suffered by my family and myself as a result. Specifically, it highlighted the events which led me to believe that our lives were in danger. It was clear to me that the INS official had reviewed the affidavit in some detail as she sought clarification on various points. Then it was over.

The only potentially controversial issue that had arisen during the interview was the possibility of my affiliation with the South African Communist Party. It was no secret that the ANC was modeled on classic left-wing liberation movements and enjoyed the support of numerous Marxist organizations, both within and without South Africa.

I was not, and never had been, a communist, I said. But the ANC was caught up in the larger East-West cold war and while the movement welcomed support from Marxist organizations and communist countries like Cuba and radical regimes like Libya, who were trying to extend their influence throughout Africa, it was essentially a nationalist organization that followed a clear "South Africa first" policy. There were of course dedicated Marxists within the ANC's ranks. Nelson Mandela was not one of them.

Mandela was always a fervent nationalist. Above all, he was a man of extraordinary integrity whose life was governed by logic, consistency and principle. As a matter of principle he refused to denounce communism after the liberation of his country from white minority rule, on the basis that communists had helped the liberation struggle when nobody else would and he was not going to turn his back on them, however distasteful such loyalty might be to some.

A month later I returned to El Paso to hear that my petition was being referred to a judge. This was a polite way of saying that the INS official did not buy my story and was handing the case to a judge who would make the final decision on my status. I was grateful for the second chance, even though it meant more trips to El Paso for more meetings with my attorney and more appearances at the INS building, only to hear each time that my case had been postponed.

But at last my attorney called. "They've set a final date. This is it. This is the real thing. You need to bring your family down with you and plan to arrive a day early so you can thoroughly prepare yourself for the court appearance."

The date was April 8, 1996, two years to the day after we had arrived in America.

The court was a drab, mid-sized room on the second floor of the INS building. We filed in and I took my place with Linda at a table below and to the right of the raised platform where the judge sat. Our attorney was with us. To our left was a similar table where three INS lawyers were busily shuffling through mounds of documents. Danielle and Lauren sat immediately behind us. For the rest of the day they would sit there, busily coloring and drawing and seemingly oblivious to their surroundings.

It hardly seemed a fitting location for an event that held such momentous importance for my family and myself. One way or another, by the end of this day our fate would be sealed.

The government case that I had reviewed with Linda in our hotel room the night before was straightforward: South Africa had undergone dramatic changes and no danger existed for us there. A 1994 report on human rights practices in South Africa noted that the country's first multiracial election in April/May of that year marked the end of 46 years of white-minority rule. Nelson Mandela was inaugurated as president on May 10. A multiparty Transitional Executive Council served as a bridge between the dissolution of the old regime and the installation of the new Government of National Unity.

While acknowledging that there continued to be credible reports of torture and unexplained deaths of persons while in police custody, the report highlighted the fact that 1994 represented a turning point in South Africa's human rights history.

"The new Interim Constitution and the Bill of Fundamental Rights provides for freedom of speech, press, assembly, association, religion, free movement of travel and domicile, and protection of minority rights. Section 29 of the Internal Security Act, which had permitted the old government to detain thousands of persons without charge or trial for indefinite periods, was repealed.

"Following the installation of the new government, there was a dramatic reduction in political and other extrajudicial killing," the report went on to note. The statesmanship and moderation exhibited by President Mandela was a major contributor towards easing tensions between the black and white communities.

In a particularly relevant passage it was noted that following the sweeping changes in the country, "asylum claims from South Africans have become increasingly rare...A few claims are based on the applicant's support of the ANC which was regarded as a terrorist organization by the previous government but a few years ago was the recipient of a broad amnesty...Since the ANC now dominates the South African Government, membership of the ANC or other opposition groups no longer would cause someone to be singled out for harassment.

"With the end of apartheid and with peaceful opposition activity now legal in South Africa, anti-apartheid activists no longer leave the country to escape arrest for their political activities."

I was troubled as I read this report, so bland in its neat generalization of events in a far-off place where once there had been strife but now all was peace and reconciliation. Turning to Linda I said, "The problem I have with this is that when I look into the mirror to shave every morning I don't see a generalization, I see me."

We sat up late into the night, rehearsing the evidence we had available to counter the INS case. One of the difficulties we faced was that we had brought so little evidence with us.

It had all been so different then, back in South Africa, back when every dawn broke with a blood-red tinge to the sky and the unbidden curdle of fear lodged in its familiar place and every hour and every street and every smile in the eyes of a stranger might herald the time and place of a cruel encounter with untimely death.

One did not make notes, then. One did not seek evidence, then, that would perhaps at some future time bolster a plea for safety in a far-off land where the sights and sounds and sensations were so different, where the very air you would breathe was charged with an impulse of freedom and safety that was all so foreign to you now. Now you simply lived day by day. Now you were a sounding board receptive to the subtle nuances of events that played their sinister tune upon you. But what machinery was there to record such a tune to provide compelling evidence on which the whole future course of your life might depend?

"All we can do is tell the truth and present what facts we have," I finally said to Linda.

I did not sleep well in the remaining hours before dawn. By the time our case began several hours later I was feeling tired and listless, hardly paying attention as the opposing lawyers presented the outlines of their cases to the judge in what was ominously termed a "Hearing in Deportation Proceedings."

Then I was called to the witness stand where I swore to tell the truth before I began answering the questions fired at me by the INS lawyers.

"They're only doing their job," I told myself. "This is not a vendetta against you, personally. It's their job to disprove your claims and it's your job not to let them."

But I felt strangely disengaged from the proceedings, as if I was viewing the whole thing through the wrong end of a telescope. It was all so unreal: America, El Paso, this courtroom, the legal maneuverings, the antiseptic questions were a million miles removed from the reality of that other place. Until one of the INS lawyers used a phrase to describe the basis for my fears that struck a chord from a half-forgotten memory. Suddenly I was galvanized by a passion that had laid dormant until now.

Once before, many years ago, I had been in a courtroom and had witnessed a horrible thing that tore at my emotions and my conscience like a knife. But in the retelling of it there was only the sound of my own voice and my uncertain convictions to convey a picture made all the more awful to witness by the casual, almost mundane way in which it had been constructed.

To a hearer at that time the fuzzy picture I recreated had been characterized as just a small event.

The phrase was unwitting existential comedy in the mindless way it trivialized the brutality that was anything but a small event to the hapless soul who experienced it and to me who witnessed it.

And here it was again, so many years later: a trivialisation of events and feelings and actual danger that could only be truly appreciated, it seemed, if they were experienced. How could I possibly convey the chilling enormity of a policeman's calculated threat, spoken on a sunny sidewalk while all about us people went about their normal business, that my children were not invulnerable to the retribution that might bypass me? How could I recount in a compelling manner the terror that consumes one, and never fully recedes after the experience, when the cold hard steel of a loaded pistol is placed against the back of the head, and the hammer is cocked, and death grins its sordid invitation? And how to explain the demons of hate that drove an Eddie Von Maltitz and his AWB friends to plot the destruction of their "kaffir-loving" enemies; demons that would not conveniently go to rest when someone signed a paper outlawing the evil system that had brought them to life?

In the context of the threats that had faced me, and I believed still faced me, it had been my ill-fortune to become an active ANC supporter in a small, ultra-conservative white community where the new order of things was vigorously opposed by some who would never accept the changes and would never forget or forgive those who had made them possible. These bitter people were the anomalies in the generally improving statistical picture of violence in South Africa, but to me they were neither anomalies nor minor statistics, they were flesh and blood threats to my very existence.

To try and drive this point home I highlighted the convenient incongruity of the government's case as it was presented to me in that drab INS courtroom. Quoting from the Human Rights Report submitted to the United States Congress at the end of 1994, one of the INS lawyers had stated that the level of political and extrajudicial killings had decreased, especially after the April election. The implication was that the danger was abating and my fears of future persecution were unfounded. Indeed, the December, 1994, total of 94 politically motivated deaths was the lowest monthly figure since February 1991.

"Like you, I'm delighted that political violence is decreasing in South Africa," I responded. "But the true implications of the numbers you have just quoted are staggering if you get away from the numbers alone and look at the actual human lives they represent.

"A little further down in the same report it gives a total of 2,687 politically motivated deaths throughout 1994, compared with 4,364 deaths the previous year. Again, that is a heartening reduction, but imagine for a moment that these 2,687 deaths occurred in America.

"Imagine the utter turmoil it would cause in a society that was so wrenched by the single assassinations of John F Kennedy and Robert F Kennedy and Dr Martin Luther King, if their deaths, in the years that they died, were multiplied 2,687 times. I wonder if America, as we know it, would survive such a thing, even though your population is ten times bigger than South Africa's, making the 2,687 number a much smaller percentage of the total number of people living in your country. And I wonder how credible would be the view expressed in the midst of such turmoil that the situation was not that bad because the number of deaths was happily showing a significant decline.

"But you might say that the deaths in South Africa were suffered by people who did not enjoy the stature of a Kennedy or a King. Well, I see here in the same report that Professor Johan Heyns was assassinated on November 5, 1994. In fact, he was gunned down at his home, in front of his family. Dr Heyns was the former head of the Dutch Reformed Church, a position within the South African context that far surpasses in stature the head of, say, the Roman Catholic Church in America.

"The report goes on to say that while the police had no suspect or confirmed motive, there was widespread speculation that rightwing extremists had assassinated Heyns for political reasons. The apparent professionalism with which the killing was carried out stunned the population and created anxiety among parliamentarians and the press about a new round of political violence.

"I want to remind you that this happened seven months after I fled South Africa. I should also point out that the small community where I lived was far more volatile than Pretoria, South Africa's capital city, where Dr Heyns lived.

"Finally, I should point out that while I in no way enjoyed the stature of a Dr Heyns, my death would have meant far more to me and my wife and my children than the cold calculation of an anomaly or a statistic."

I had spoken with passion, with conviction, and I knew that my arguments were hitting home. But by this time I had been over four hours on the witness stand and I was tired. Thankfully, the INS lawyers asked me only a few more questions before indicating that their examination of me was complete.

Then it was Linda's turn. Although she was not the petitioner in this case my lawyer felt it would be useful for her to give her perspective. The INS lawyers immediately attacked the seeming lack of any real deprivation she had suffered as a result of my activities and the alleged threats against me.

Here was the wife of a wealthy man, who had lived in a large high-end home where she enjoyed the services of two maids and a gardener to complement the ease and comfort of a lifestyle which had undergone little or no evident change, right up until the time she left South Africa. Surely this indicated that the so-called threats were not real?

Linda appeared so small and vulnerable on the witness stand, but her slight frame and petite features were deceptive. Her underlying strength of character had been honed by the years of uncertainty and ever-present sense of danger that came from living in a small border town where the usual political turmoil and social unrest was given a personal significance by my political activities. She was a lot tougher than she seemed.

She answered the questions firmly and clearly, making the point again and again that the outward appearance of her life was but one side of a cloth that also carried a somber pattern of increasing fear and insecurity.

She owed it to her children and to her husband, she said, to maintain as far as possible a semblance of normalcy. She refused to give in to her own fears, although it was difficult at times to maintain this resolve.

The INS lawyer would not let go of his line of questioning.

"Mrs. Thal," he said politely, "I put it to you that you were never in any real danger. You never suffered any direct threats. Neither you nor your children nor your husband ever suffered any actual physical harm. You have presented no evidence to the contrary and yet you want this court to believe that the danger you were in was sufficient to cause you to flee."

Linda paused for a moment to digest this statement. Then she turned slowly and deliberately to the judge and spoke in a quiet yet firm voice: "It seems to me that we will never be able to prove what was real to us. The only evidence I can present is that I left all that was near and dear to me - my mother, my close friends, my beautiful home, my dreams of a peaceful retirement in the land that I loved, surrounded by my grandchildren - I left it all, not on a whim, but because I was terrified of what could happen to me or to my family at any moment."

She paused again, and then she added, tearfully this time, "My family and I paid a price in fear and uncertainty before coming to America. But it seems the only evidence that would be acceptable to this court would be to present the dead body of my husband as

188

proof of the danger we were in. That, however, remains a price higher than I am willing to pay."

There was a lengthy hush in the courtroom. Then the judge glanced at the lawyers and back at Linda before declaring that he had heard enough testimony. He would shortly deliver his ruling, he said, before leaving the room.

When he returned after what were only a few minutes, but seemed like an eternity, the judge called me back into the witness stand and began a slow and methodical presentation of the contents and application of the law as it applied to requests for political asylum. He outlined what he could and could not do as the final arbiter of the evidence before him. While his careful voice droned on I stood transfixed. The realization had suddenly come to me in all of its horrifying force that in the next few seconds or minutes I would hear a pronouncement that might plunge my family and I into a vortex whose end was so terrible as to not bear imagining. If the judge ruled against us we would immediately be taken from the court to gather up our small possessions in Albuquerque before being placed on a flight back to South Africa. The law called for this to happen within 24 hours, which seemed like almost indecent haste after the months and months of waiting to hear the determination of our fate.

I knew in that moment what it felt like to be a death row inmate and hear the cell door clang open for the last time as the execution date dawned. Feelings of terror, helplessness and resignation washed over me in equal measure.

Then the judge seemed to gather himself and take a deeper breath as he turned to me.

189

"It is the pronouncement of this court," he said, "that the respondent has satisfied the requirements of the law pertaining to a request for asylum. The court therefore orders that the respondent's application for asylum under Section 208 (a) of the Immigration and Nationality Act is hereby granted. Furthermore, it is ordered that deportation proceedings be terminated. Appeal is waived by all parties."

As the words fell on my unbelieving ears the pent-up tension from years of uncertainty and fear exploded from me in an almost animal-like cry of release. I could not contain myself. I was beyond embarrassment. My emotions, held in check for so long by an iron resolve, would no longer be stayed. I wept as if my heart had broken.

The rest of courtroom sat in stunned silence. Then Linda began to cry as the import of the moment settled on her. Our poor children, so obedient and well-behaved all day long because they had been told that this was a very, very special day, watched in confusion as their parents cried and then they cried too.

Linda turned to console them and then she walked to where I sat and hugged me. Our lawyer came across and hugged us both. Then, unbelievably, the INS lawyers came over to shake our hands. At last it was the turn of the judge.

"Congratulations," he said quietly, as he turned to leave the room.

It was over.

We were home.

CHAPTER TWELVE
Perspective

Time is a wonderful healer. It is also a thief that robs us of youth and innocence. The loss of innocence with regard to my perspective on America has come hard.

First there have been the conflicting emotions of gratitude and frustration surrounding my family's status. We consider ourselves very fortunate to have found safety in a country with a heart as big as the Statue of Liberty, even as we linger in helpless uncertainty, year after year, while the grinding wheels of bureaucracy process our application for permanent residence following our successful appeal for political asylum.

Happily, the wait has not prevented us from breaking free of our early employment difficulties. I established a successful business while Linda pursued a professional career as a chemical analyst. Our daughters have blossomed into delightful teenagers little different from their many American friends, with no outward signs of the traumatic circumstances that brought them here. Yet we still have to apply annually for authorization to work and neither Linda nor I enjoy the legal status that easily allows us to enter into binding contracts, or to buy or sell property. In a sense, we're non-persons.

And then there has been the discomfort of adjusting to the reality of political life in America. It took a single event, the abduction of Elian Gonzalez from a home in Florida, to shatter my notions about the unassailable superiority of the American political

191

system. I am still struggling to come to terms with the horrific images surrounding this extraordinary action.

Indeed, my only flash of true fear since arriving in America was the moment I saw the all too familiar picture of jackbooted, helmeted, heavily armed stormtroopers crashing into a private home and snatching a terrified child out of the arms of a cowed adult. I had witnessed this awful scene in the bleak place of ruthless oppression that was once my home, but to see it happen in America was incomprehensible to me. Equally incomprehensible was the muted protest from most Americans.

There are those who explain that the event was made necessary by the intransigent behavior of the Florida Cubans, and those who say it was made possible by a strange love affair that the liberal establishment pursues with the Stalinist Fidel Castro. But after living so many years in a police state and now enjoying all the freedoms that America confers, the silence is still mystifying. Equally mystifying is the seemingly endless stream of American celebrities and left-wing politicians being wined and dined by their friend Fidel and singing the praises of his cynically repressive regime.

So America has warts. Viewed against the background of where I have come from this country is a paradise, but it is clearly a paradise troubled by seductive and poisonous elements no less dangerous than the serpent that beguiled Eve. On the other hand, South Africa - for all its hellish aspects - was not all bad. As I mulled over the Gonzalez incident I was reminded of two minor events I experienced in South Africa and America that provided at once a remarkable illustration of their differences and similarities, underlining the natural complexity of both societies and the significance within them of small actions, decisions and simple nuances that are part of a larger tapestry.

The incidents that came to mind both involved children, who are the passive receptors of today's prejudices and the active shapers of tomorrow's new icons and shibboleths. In the first, South African experience, it was a sunny weekday morning as I walked down the main street of my home-town with its usual complement of half a dozen vehicles and perhaps twice as many pedestrians going about their unhurried business. A few paces ahead of me on the sidewalk were two small white boys, perhaps ten or eleven years old. Coming towards us was a middle-aged black man dressed in a laborer's overalls, his eyes in the customary downcast position. The boys held to their course in the center of the sidewalk and as he came up to them the black man moved to one side, letting them pass. As payment for his deferential action he received from the bigger of the two boys a sneering laugh and the words, "Stupid kaffir!"

The man gave no sign that he had heard the spiteful greeting, but I was appalled - not so much by the words, which were commonplace - but by the unthinking arrogance in children so young. Grabbing the black man by the arm as he came up to me, I asked him to stop and then took a few quick paces that allowed me to place my hands on the scruff of both white necks. Turning the boys towards me I glared first at one and then the other.

"You little men are going to learn an important lesson today," I told them.

Fear and confusion were mirrored on both faces as I hustled them towards the black man standing a few feet away. Squirming in my grip the bigger boy asked plaintively, "What's wrong, sir? What have we done?"

"What you've done is to disrespect your elders," I said. "You were rude to this man and now you're going to apologize to him."

A look of blank incomprehension met my statement.

"But sir, he's a kaffir!"

"No! He's older than you. He's older than your father. And you must learn to respect those who are older than you. Your must learn good manners."

But the incomprehension was total and the child could only repeat, a tear in his voice this time, "He's a kaffir. You can't make me say sorry to a kaffir."

"Yes I can. And you will. You were rude to him and you must say sorry."

The next response frightened me because its immutable logic reflected the measure of South Africa's pain and the impossible heights of its distress.

"No, you can't make me say sorry," the boy sniveled, crying freely now. "My Pa won't let me say sorry to a kaffir."

"Why not?" I retorted.

"A kaffir is a dog." the boy replied.

"No!" I cried again. "This is not a dog. He is a man like me, like your father, like your grandfather."

"He's a dog!" the boy replied, now defiant. "I'm going to tell my father and he's going to beat you because you want me to say sorry to a dog."

I could feel my anger rising and I increased my pressure on the boy's neck as I said to him through gritted teeth, "Listen, sonny. My name is Phillip Thal. I work at B.T. Wholesalers.

You can send your Pa to me any time you like, but right now you're going to say sorry to this man for your rudeness to him."

With that I shoved him towards the spot where the black man had been standing. But he was gone. Startled, I looked down the sidewalk and saw the man several yards away, walking stiffly from a scene that was not only embarrassing to him but had the unmistakable signs of an event that experience had taught would ultimately make him the recipient of the white man's censure, or worse. Frustration rose like bile in my throat. I could not illustrate my point to these children if the main character in the little drama was an unwilling player, and so I lectured them briefly once more on the necessity for good manners, regardless of race, then let them go.

The next morning shortly after I opened my warehouse for business a white man in his mid-thirties knocked tentatively on my office door and asked to speak to me.

He introduced himself as Johan Prinsloo.

"You met my boy yesterday," he said. "That thing with the black man. I came to say thank you."

I was momentarily at a loss for words. I had foreseen the possibility of an angry confrontation with the parents of both boys, but this was wholly unexpected. Reacting to my obvious confusion, the man continued, his voice soft but firm: "There is a lot of ugliness in our country. I am trying to teach my son

195

that all people have dignity and worth. I am trying to teach him how to think so that the ugliness all around him does not make his soul ugly. But it is very hard. His friends…"

The man shrugged his shoulders as his voice trailed off. There was nothing more to say. We both understood. With a rush of something approaching elation I reached out and shook his hand. The realization had come to me while he was speaking that he was the father of the smaller of the two boys, the one who had not spoken throughout the incident the previous day.

"Mr. Prinsloo," I said warmly, "I should thank you. As difficult as your position is, I want to reassure you that it is the right one; and as isolated as you may feel, you should know that as long as there is one Johan Prinsloo left in South Africa, there is hope for our country."

We parted company after a few minutes of further conversation. Despite an open invitation to visit my home or my business at any time, I never saw him again. A few months later I fled South Africa, but the memory of Johan Prinsloo and his simple decency is with me still. I wonder where he and his son are today.

About a year after coming to America I had an equally disturbing experience involving a child and his father. Although this latter event did not have racial connotations it nevertheless spoke volumes for what is happening in this country, and perhaps where our future lies.

It was a Saturday and I was skiing on Albuquerque's Sandia Peak, the 10,000 foot tall mountain that rises abruptly like a massive

196

exclamation from its roots in the nearby Rio Grande. As I rode a chairlift my attention was drawn to the chair immediately ahead of me, where a small boy was holding a snowball that he obviously intended to hurl at the skiers passing some forty feet below us.

"Hey!" I called out. "Don't do that. You could hurt somebody."

But I was too late. The boy let fly with the snowball, which struck a startled skier on the shoulder. I craned my head to see the man looking around in confusion as he brushed the snow from his jacket. He did not think to look up.

Turning my attention back to the boy, I noted with alarm that he was now banging his skis together to knock the snow off them onto those below us. While the small amount of snow that fell was not a danger, there was the more threatening possibility that the rough treatment could knock off one of his skis, sending a deadly missile onto an unprotected head far below.

"Hey!" I yelled again. "Stop that!"

But the boy paid no attention and continued crashing his skis together. A man sitting next to him turned briefly to identify the source of the shouting and then offered me his back once more. Minutes later we arrived at the crest of the ski run and the pair ahead of me moved off onto the slope. I skied quickly up to the boy and planted myself in his path.

"Hello, son." I said mildly. "I want you to know that what you did back there was very dangerous."

The child, whom I estimated to be about ten years old, gave me a blank stare. I was about to say something more when the man who had been on the lift with him came up to us.

"What are you doing to my boy?" he demanded angrily.

Smiling at the man and extending my hand to him I asked the obvious question, "Is this your son?"

Ignoring my proffered handshake he bluntly replied, "Yes. What do you want with him?"

"Well, sir, he's a fine looking boy, but I wanted him to know that what he did back there on the chairlift was dangerous and he should not do it again. Somebody could have been seriously hurt."

The man gave me a withering stare. Then between clenched teeth he hissed, "What my son does is no damn business of yours. Now get out of here before I whip your ass!"

I ignored the threat and keeping my voice as even as possible, I said to him, "Actually, sir, it is my business. What your son did was dangerous and it could have been me or one of my children beneath him on that slope. That's why I'm making it my business. All I'm asking of you and your boy is to recognize the danger so that he doesn't do that again. I'm sure your son did not mean to hurt anybody, but good intentions are no substitute for good behavior."

Now the man looked incredulous. "What the hell are you talking about? Of course he didn't hurt anybody. So what's your point?"

"My point is that the fact he did not hurt anybody does not excuse his actions. He needs to know that he could have hurt somebody. He needs to know that wrong actions may have unhappy results."

Now red in the face, his voice rising, the father spat at me, "Look, mister, I don't know who you are and I don't know where you come from, but I'm warning you to back off. Leave my son alone. Stop trying to scare him."

Now it was my turn to be incredulous. The situation was spiraling out of control and not for the first time I wondered why I was so prone to stirring controversy with even the best intentions. Taking a deep breath I looked squarely at the unhappy father and said quietly to him, "I'm sorry, sir. I'll back off, like you say. But I can't walk away without asking you to consider that the day might come when your boy does something that causes you or someone else a lot of grief, and you will be left asking yourself the question, 'Where did I go wrong?'

"Then I want you to remember this day. This is it. This is where you go wrong. This is where you miss the opportunity to teach your child some responsibility, teach him how to behave in a society where his actions affect other people, instead of treating him like cotton candy."

With that, I turned abruptly and threw myself down the slope. I did not look back.

Two events. Two societies. Two very different circumstances. Both equally troubling for what they reveal about little patterns of behavior, little deeds and little things undone, little attitudes flowing together that shape our collective destiny. Ultimately, they will be reflected on a larger scale in tragic events or heroic deeds that stir a nation. The law of unintended consequences is immutable.

It is this that troubles me so deeply about something like the easy acceptance of the Gonzalez abduction and the related sycophancy surrounding Fidel Castro: what are the roots of these attitudes, and where will they lead?

Similarly, I am troubled and mystified by America's seemingly blind descent into a minefield of warring camps that must ultimately tear this great nation apart. It is a phenomenon that appears to be gaining strength and it holds enormous implications, but there seems to be little substantive debate on the matter.

Nowhere is this more graphically illustrated than in the area of race. Never in my wildest dreams would I have expected to find apartheid alive and well in the United States, and that it would be promoted by black people. The whole idea is quite bizarre, but real nevertheless.

The evidence of it is everywhere, from black names for people who live in black cities, to all-black schools and totally segregated universities like Cornell, to black congressional districts, to black employment quotas and a black Christmas called Kwanza, a fabrication with only the most tenuous links to Africa, whose chief merit seems to be the fact that it separates blacks from whites at a time of year that traditionally brings people together.

Perhaps nothing defines this apartheid more than the very term, African-American, which immediately sets black people apart from all other Americans. Of course, it's not called apartheid here - the new buzzword is multiculturalism - but to me it looks like the same old thing in new clothes.

I fear that the end of multiculturalism will be a division into exclusive, hostile camps through the creation of different "tribes" who will not see themselves as Americans first but as members of special interest groups competing for a slice of the American pie. Ultimately there will be no pie for anyone. One has only to look at the violence and turmoil that still tears South Africa apart so many years after the official death of apartheid, to see the unintended consequences of a policy that says we can only fully enjoy what is ours if someone else is excluded from our enjoyment of it.

I have no doubt that because multiculturalism is a peculiar American form of a thoroughly discredited ideology it will eventually fail here for the same reason it failed in South Africa: those who bear its burden will simply refuse to put up with it any longer.

Unfortunately, as in South Africa, a lot of people will be spiritually, emotionally and economically impoverished before that glad day comes.

And when the denouement arrives the cultural elite who gave multiculturalism form and substance will be exposed, not as a fanatical bunch of conservative white South Africans who believed they were fulfilling a divine commission, but as a liberal white establishment who should have known better but were dazzled by light of their own brilliance. The liberal elite who influence so much of America's perceptions through their stranglehold on schools, universities and the media have bought into the idea of multiculturalism in a big way, and in the process they confer sainthood on anyone who emerges as the leader of the next trendy cause that may give birth to a new cultural tribe. In the case of a well-established, easily identifiable tribe like black Americans, sainthood is conferred on all who share the same skin color - just as those crazies in South Africa once believed about whites.

The parrallells with South Africa are everywhere I look; it's just that in America everything is in reverse. So it is that a South African leader like Nelson Mandela is a healer of the breach between black and white while his American equivalent - a Jesse Jackson or an Al Sharpton - is a promoter of the breach.

Mandela has spent his whole life - and I mean spent in the sense of sacrifice - to advance the cause of his people in particular, and his nation in general. His every action testifies to his patriotism, his love for South Africa, and in particular, his desire to heal the rifts between black and white. But compare his record and his utterances to those of some American leaders who would like to be seen as his "brothers" but aren't worthy to shine his shoes.

National figures like Jesse Jackson and Al Sharpton are hustlers whose unfettered bigotry and race-baiting are disgraceful tools of their pan-handling trade. There is no comparison between them and Mandela. They're absolutely cynical in the way they pervert and manipulate the inconsistencies that are a part of any open society in an effort to promote their narrow agendas. They'll pounce on any opportunity to divide rather than heal.

The difference between them and Mandela is simply that in place of his logic, consistency and principle, they have only shallow expediency. Mandela paid a very high price for his beliefs without ever compromising, but after his release from 27 years in one of the world's most brutal prison systems, he was gracious and forgiving to his enemies and warm and generous to his friends. He could have triggered a bloodbath in South Africa by denouncing his captors, and whites in general; instead, he chose the path of reconciliation and reconstruction. History will long celebrate him for his statesmanship.

But what will Jackson and others of his stripe be remembered for? So many black leaders are dangerous to the future of every black person in America, not so much for their greedy exploitation of white guilt but for the fact that they have been able to build a power base only by differentiating their constituency from mainstream America in every way possible. It is a form of reverse apartheid quite sickening in its brazen execution.

A charitable explanation might be that black people see their strength in numbers and unite around issues of particular interest to them, but surely the phenomenon is supportable only if we are considering first or even second generation immigrants to this country? What's the logic for it after hundreds of years? The genius of America has always been its ability to assimilate, not divide - integration, not segregation, is the norm.

It would of course be foolish to pretend that racial integration has been a smooth process, or that racism is not an ugly fact of life in America today. But surely the way to eliminate racism is to mute the differences between people, not accentuate them? Like Nelson Mandela, Dr Martin Luther King had a dream in which all Americans regardless of skin color shared together the bounty which America offers.

This breakdown in American unity is a disturbing fact so at odds with all the marvelous outer trappings of her culture and her history that make her so great, such a beacon to the oppressed masses of the world. American symbols like the Declaration of Independence, the Constitution, the Gettysburg Address and the Statue of Liberty represent a truth and a vision infinitely superior to anything else this world has to offer. They have a dynamic life all of their own.

Yet they hide a multitude of America's sins.

The awful truth that lurks behind the facade that these symbols present is that many Americans don't believe in them any more. They don't even believe in themselves as Americans any more. Instead, they have come to believe in themselves as self-actualized individuals. But how long can a nation of selfish individuals endure?

I want to be an American because I believe passionately in America. I believe in her great institutions and the great principles that are the bedrock on which she is founded. What's more, I'm especially proud to be an immigrant who believes these things because I'm coming to understand that it may be the great huddled masses who flock to these shores in pursuit of the American dream who may ultimately be the hope of America. Americans themselves may be losing the vision, but it is our privilege to breathe life into it again. Every time an immigrant falls in love with America, that enthusiasm for her greatness is a down payment on ensuring her survival.

It's ironic that a nation of immigrants who have lost their way may be saved from self-destruction by yet more immigrants. This is my hope.

Perhaps the reality that is America today lies somewhere yet to be discovered, somewhere in the arcane depths that make up the American soul. But until that discovery is made, I'll happily sign onto the thought that as a newcomer here my enjoyment of all that is uniquely American may indeed contribute to ultimately preserving all that is uniquely American.

And as the process unfolds I will continue to be enormously grateful.

To be alive.

To be here.

To be free.

Hugo Thal

EPILOGUE
Minnesota Winter

The hardwood forest wore its heavy weight of snow like a festive bride at the wedding of some fabled king. Oak, aspen, ash, elm, birch and maple, an occasional errant spruce, undergrowth and brush, all naked and dressed again in white on brilliant white; each trunk, branch, stick and twig a stark black exclamation etched in lattice and lace.

The silence was immense. Sound itself lay captive to the ice and snow and overhanging cloud. When the snow fell again it came without fanfare, floating flat and moist, until the air itself seemed to exhale a gently roiling froth.

At a bend in a narrow trail marked by the delicate spiked imprints of fleeting deer, I stood watching, sensing more than seeing the snow breathing through the snow white trees, gathering my own soft mantle, conscious only of the probing cold and a single startling splash of red that confronted me like a damning eye. The blood was harsh and out of place; here, in all this white, in all this pristine softness, the blood did not belong. It was an alien thing. Accusing me.

I turned slowly, hearing the soft crunch of snow beneath my feet. Back there along the trail lay another splash, already made translucent pink by brushing flakes that seemed intent on hiding all evidence of my guilt. I turned again, and pressed on. Ahead somewhere a deer was wounded, and I had to find it, had to complete an act that started in a rush of glee as three deer crossed my path and I raised the expectant rifle to my shoulder, sighted through the scope, squeezed the shot, felt the barrel kick, heard the spiteful crash, saw the bullet hit. But the deer would not stay down. I watched in fascination as it stumbled, staggered, crumpled, stood again, fell once more, burdened by a foreign weight, then gasped and rose and bounded down the trail, its white tail waving like a flag that mocked my sudden impotence.

And now, all pleasure gone, I plodded slowly forward. Here, another gleaming spot, and there, another. Like neon beacons pointing they drew me slowly on, rifle heavy in my arms, cold comfort in my bones. I had discovered in this single swift act of violence a hidden deep revulsion at the thought of death, of killing. There was so much blood clinging to my soul, from my association with a past in a place so far removed from this white wilderness; so much from a history that I could not deny but could surely try to forget.

All around the silent sylvan forest listened to my thoughts.

I paused, checked my compass, checked my watch. Incredibly, only ten minutes had passed since the shot, but it seemed much longer. The day was long. I had been up since sunrise and now it was well past noon. My presence here followed an invitation from Steven to celebrate the victory of my reprieve with an experience so utterly different from anything I had seen or done in Africa: deer hunting in the Minnesota winter woods. I had jumped at the chance. But now I could take no pleasure from the taste of it.

Then the sun broke through the heavy cloud and suddenly the forest was transformed by mottled light that gleamed like Day-Glo on the snow. Heartened by this friendly omen I shuffled on, carefully skirting a leaning bush made heavy by its load of white. And then I saw it.

The deer lay still, stretched on its side. I moved beside it, leaning on my rifle, then prodded it softly with my boot. A long moment passed. Falling slowly to my knees I reached to my side and drew the knife, placing the steel tip gently on the deer's white belly. I bowed my head and tried to say a prayer an ancient hunter might have said when finding food that would sustain him. But this hunter was well fed. The prayer died on my lips. I could not kill the deer again, already dead.

Suddenly I stood and in a shambling haste I gathered brush and snow, determined that the deer would not be found by some other passerby, determined it would not leave there but stay wedded to the forest that would reclaim its small remains when the season turned. At last my job was done and I backed slowly from the ragged mound, brushing footprint traces and all sign of blood and struggle.

I took a last long look and then I turned and headed back down the trail. An hour later I found the truck parked at the forest's edge, my three hunting companions gathered there.

"Any luck?" one asked.

"No," I said. "I didn't see a thing."

ADDENDUM

Extracts from an Amnesty International Report on South Africa. Covering events from January to December, 2000.

"There were reports of ill-treatment, torture and unjustified use of lethal force by police and security forces..."

"Continuing official and public concern at levels of violent crime, large-scale circulation of illegal weapons and a spate of bombings in the Cape Town area led to a number of high profile joint military and police security operations in different parts of the country."

"The South African Law Commission issued an interim report on a proposed anti-terrorism bill, which contained provisions for prolonged detention without charge for interrogation of individuals believed to have information on terrorist acts."

"Four police officers were charged with murder and released on bail in connection with the suspected extrajudicial execution of an ANC parliamentarian, Bheki Mhkize, in July. He was shot dead when about a dozen members of the Public Order Unit based at Ulundi in KwaZulu Natal raided his home, apparently searching for weapons. Independent forensic and other evidence gathered by the ICD (Independent Complaints Directorate) indicated that he was shot intentionally at close range by the police."

"Human rights lawyers and members of investigation bodies were subjected to physical attack, death threats or other forms of harassment as a consequence of their work."

"In July an ICD investigator, Velaphi Kwela, was killed on his way to carry out an arrest. He was shot seven times and thrown out of his vehicle."

"In September magistrate Pieter Theron, who was hearing a case against PAGAD members, was killed in a drive-by shooting outside his home in Cape Town."

Hugo Thal

ABOUT THE AUTHOR

Phillip Thal took a stand against the oppressive white regime in the Apartheid era of South Africa. This is his story.

Edward Thal is a former marketing executive who now lives in the Washington D.C. area where he teaches in a private Christian School.

The two brothers shared a common disdain for the political structure in South Africa. They have collaborated on this harrowing story to provide a shocking insight to a time and a place once heralded as a bastion of white civilization.

Printed in the United States
768800001B